A CHRISTMAS ROMANCE

The way Greg was talking, as if he could solve all her problems . . . Julia almost smiled. Even if it was the magic of Christmas, Greg had made some things nicer.

She put her hand on his arm, unable to help herself. At that moment he reached out and, without any warning, pulled her to him.

"Julia," he said desperately, "now that you know what I do at the bank, I'm not going to let you struggle alone out here. I'm going to—" He was staring into her eyes, unable to come up with adequate words. "I'm going to *kiss* you."

To his surprise, she didn't pull away. But it was a kiss that neither of them had really expected. He had wanted to go slow—at least in the beginning. But what had happened was entirely different. It was a kiss full of yearning and desire. With that one simple, innocent kiss, it was possible their lives had changed completely . . . .

"Celebrate the Christmas season with a warm, wondrous romance, full of magic and joy, courtesy of . . . Maggie Daniels!"

—*Romantic Times*

A Christmas ROMANCE

MAGGIE DANIELS

ST. MARTIN'S PAPERBACKS

For Maureen O'Neal

A CHRISTMAS ROMANCE

Copyright © 1991 by Maggie Davis.

ISBN: 0-312-92669-3

Printed in the United States of America

St. Martin's Paperbacks edition/December 1991

10 9 8 7 6 5 4 3 2

Famous Stonecypher Family Recipe Pecan Pound Cake

1/2 pound butter
2 1/2 cups sugar
6 eggs
3 cups sifted
  cake flour
2 teaspoons
  baking powder
1 teaspoon salt
1 teaspoon
  ground nutmeg
1 cup sour cream
1/2 cup bourbon
1 1/2 cups
  chopped pecans

GLAZE
2 cups sifted
  confectioners'
  sugar
1 tablespoon
  bourbon (or
  bourbon-
  flavored
  extract)
2 tablespoons
  water

Preheat oven to 325°F. Combine butter and sugar; beat until light and fluffy. Add eggs one at a time, beating constantly. Sift dry ingredients together. Blend sour cream and bourbon. Combine flour and sour cream mixtures alternately. Add pecans. Grease bottom and sides of tube or bundt pan. Pour in batter. Bake for 1 hour and 15 minutes (test for doneness by inserting a cake tester or knife; this cake may need an extra 15 minutes). Cool in pan for 15 minutes, then turn out on wire rack. Stir glaze ingredients together and pour over warm cake.

One

THE MAN FROM THE BANK WAS BACK AGAIN.
From her front window, Julia watched the sleek white Cutlass Ciera cross the river and the snow-covered bridge, thinking: I'll have to tell him I've lost my job. And that I'll catch up with all the payments after New Year's.

That makes November *and* December rent you can't pay for, Julia's inner voice warned her, and maybe January. He's not going to like that.

The new loan officer from the Dalton bank had replaced nice old Mr. Harding, who had retired in the fall. A few weeks ago, when he'd made his first trip to Makim's Mountain, the new loan man had made it clear that for Julia to be temporarily out of money was nothing short of immoral. She still cringed when she thought of it. Being financially strapped was no excuse, he'd lectured her, one had to save, regardless, to meet one's obligations.

And if bank payments were due, one had a sacred obligation to pay on time. No matter what. He'd been very firm about that.

Well, Julia decided, taking a deep breath, she could be firm, too. Because there just wasn't any money. It was going to be a tight enough Christmas anyway, with just one gift apiece for the girls, but they couldn't afford anything more. As for the overdue rent—the bank officer had made his trip up the mountain two days before Christmas for nothing. She wasn't going to let anybody or anything spoil what could be their last holiday there.

Outside, the snow was falling steadily. The road was almost covered. By the time the Cutlass made the second curve, it was fishtailing across the half-frozen dirt. Typical city driver, Julia thought. None of them ever really learned how to drive on red clay mountain roads.

She rested her forehead against the window glass, telling herself once again there was no reason on earth to think that once disaster struck it would keep on happening. But it seemed that nothing had gone right since that horrible night two years ago when James Stonecypher had been removed from his loving family by a Makim's Mountain summer visitor driving a Cadillac. Who hadn't seen Jim's motorcycle in time.

Losing Jim had gradually become a faint ache, not the terrible knifelike pain it had once been, but that still didn't make it any better. She'd had two whole years of unforgiving grief that had, eventually, been bad for Deenie and Emily Rose. And bad for herself.

"Mother?" It was Deenie coming across the living room with a green and red Christmas paper chain looped carefully over both hands. "We've used up all the glue," she announced, "and there isn't any more. But you don't have to worry. I know how to make some with flour, like they used to do in the old days. They showed us in craft class in school." She looked past Julia to the window. "Oh, Mother, it's snowing! Do you think they'll close the bridge? Wouldn't it be wonderful if we had a big snow for Christmas and we had all the mountain just to ourselves?"

Julia couldn't help smiling. Her older child had the solemn expression of all children who wore eyeglasses and resembled the Makims, Julia's side of the family, with Julia's big, dark eyes, and way of smiling. She was not at all like her younger sister, Emily Rose, who was bound, everyone agreed, to grow up beautiful enough to devastate every male within spitting distance.

"Wonderful that it's going to snow before I can get to town?" Julia kept her eye on the automobile making its way up the mountain road. "Deenie, I've still got all my Christmas cakes to deliver!"

Her daughter suddenly threw both arms around her. "It's going to be a good Christmas, Mommy. Don't worry about anything. I'll help you wrap the pound cakes and deliver them before the snow gets too deep. And even if we're snowed in," she ended determinedly, "we'll have a *white Christmas,* won't we?"

Julia hugged her back affectionately. "Honey, what am I going to do with you? A white Christmas? Are you going to help me shovel tons of snow off the car? And a path out to the barn and the driveway, and all the things like that?"

"Yes." Deenie buried her face in Julia's sweater. "I love you, Mother," she said, her voice muffled. "I just don't want you to worry."

Julia stroked her daughter's fine, dark hair, drawn into two ponytails that hung over each ear. The past two years hadn't been easy, especially for Deenie. Since her father's death, she hadn't given up any of her babyhood fantasies. At nine, she still believed stubbornly in fairies and Winnie the Pooh and, of course, Santa Claus. As her school grades showed, she spent far too much time daydreaming.

"I'm not worrying, honey," Julia said hurriedly. The bank officer's auto was almost there. "But if you're going to help me wrap cakes you'd better get started. I'll be with you just as soon as I go for the mail."

Going for the mail meant she could meet the bank officer in the driveway and keep him outside where the children would, hopefully, not even see him. Even though it was almost Christmas Eve, some cards might still be arriving, along with a late order for a Famous Stonecypher Family Recipe Pecan Pound Cake. Since Jim's death, the cakes had supplied ready money. And the demand was extra high at the holidays.

As she stepped off the front porch, the bitter cold snatched Julia's breath away. She grabbed her old cardigan sweater around her, thinking the temperature must be dropping crazily; she

4

couldn't remember it ever getting so cold so fast, and she had lived on Makim's Mountain all her life. The tip of her nose was numb before she was halfway to the mailbox.

From the driveway one could see the four miles down Makim's Mountain Road to the curve before the bridge. The iron span, built sixty years ago when there were many more farms and farmers in north Georgia, had been targeted for years by the state highway department for replacement. These days it was so rickety the county road crews usually closed it down at the first sign of bad weather.

The bank officer's car was just taking the last curve before the house, going a little too fast on the frozen dirt. As she watched, the Cutlass skidded, failed to make the turn at the driveway, and stopped, angled out into the road.

Julia took a deep breath. Remember Christmas, she told herself, and goodwill to men. Even this one. The best she could offer was a promise that somehow she'd catch up on the November and December rent in the new year.

The man inside the car opened the door and tested the red clay with the tip of one carefully polished shoe, muttering something under his breath about getting these confounded roads paved. Then he got out.

"Mrs. Stonecypher?" The new loan officer was several inches over six feet and wore an expensive cashmere overcoat and gold-rimmed glasses. He was fairly young, probably not much over thirty, Julia thought, and he was probably the handsomest man she'd seen in a long time, with his tawny, slightly waving hair, determined chin, and penetrating blue eyes. But his good looks didn't seem to make him happy; his wide mouth was clamped tight, and two grooves between his dark brows indicated he frowned quickly and often. Snowflakes settled in his hair immediately. He lifted his hand to brush at them, annoyed. "I'm Gregory Harding, vice-president of the Dalton Bank and Trust Company. You remember I—"

"Yes," Julia said quickly. She didn't want him to come any farther; if he came up on the porch she'd have to invite him inside. She didn't want her girls to hear anything about unpaid rent. "It wasn't really necessary for you to come all the way up the mountain today, Mr. Harding," she said, a little breathlessly, "because I'm going to have to send the bank this month's and last month's rent sometime after Christmas."

The frown on his face was quickly replaced by a disdainful expression that said he never believed a word anyone told him. At least the first time around.

"I should have told you the bad news as early as Halloween," Julia said, trying to sound even more apologetic. She hugged the sweater around her. "Even back at Halloween it looked as though we were going to have a hard time getting through the holidays, the girls and I, even worse than last year. So I had to cut back paying some bills—some *important* bills," she added, remembering the notice from the heating oil company. "I'm sorry, but I just don't have the money. I had to save something back for Christmas."

He stared at her, disbelieving. "You knew in *October*," he said finally, biting off each word, "that you weren't going to make your payments? So you decided to skip them? To hold back something for *Christmas*?"

Good heavens, he could even make "Christmas" sound like a dirty word. "I have two little girls to take care of, Mr. Harding. I have to see that they have enough to eat, and proper clothes so they can go to school. Besides, Christmas is important to us!"

His expression grew even more incredulous. "You can't make your payments because you won't have any money for *Christmas*? Good lord, you people up here in the mountains have got to start living in the twentieth century! Talk about ignorant and backward—"

He stopped. His eyes moved over Julia, taking in her blowing hair, the way she clutched the inadequate old sweater to her. One corner of his mouth quirked cynically.

"Mrs. Stonecypher, I hope it doesn't come as too much of a surprise to you, but the bank no longer wishes to continue my uncle's lenient policy that allowed you to pay rent on property already in the possession of the bank at your husband's death."

Reluctantly, Julia nodded. The bank *had* been lenient—at least up to the time the older Mr. Harding had retired. When Grandpa Stonecypher died, his homeplace was so debt-ridden it had been almost impossible to pay its way free and clear, but she and Jim had tried. Still, the bank took it over anyway. It had been more than kind and generous of old Mr. Harding to let her rent the house until she got back on her feet after Jim's death. The only problem was getting back on her feet when she'd really never been on her feet to begin with.

"You've known for over two years," the loan officer was saying, "that this property is earmarked for condominium development and has a construction timetable to meet. The bank can't allow this situation to drift any longer."

Yes, she knew about the condominiums. Resorts were springing up in the north Georgia mountains all the way to Tennessee. It took some getting used to, the way people were coming in; especially when a family like hers, the Makims, had been on one mountain for so long they'd given their name to it.

"Drift?" Julia said cautiously. "What does that mean?"

He made an impatient sound between his teeth, eyes narrowed. Under that look Julia flushed. She was wearing jeans and a frayed shirt under the sweater; she supposed she didn't look as smart and pretty as most women he dealt with.

"It's unavoidable," he said, reaching inside his coat and pulling out a paper, "that notices come due at the fiscal quarter. That is, right at the holidays." He added, "I'm sorry."

Julia took the paper. For no reason at all she suddenly had a wild, foolish thought that maybe someone at the bank—perhaps the other, nicer, retired Mr. Harding—was going to do something for her and the girls at Christmas. Right when they needed it.

"Oh, thank you," she murmured. She turned the envelope around, almost afraid to open it. Maybe it said, *Merry Christmas! All of us at the Dalton Bank and Trust Co. have decided to give you until February to catch up with your past due payments.* "If the bank could just give me more time," Julia said gratefully, "I'd really appreciate it. You see, I . . . I lost my job Friday. I haven't had the heart to tell my girls. I thought I'd wait until Christmas was over."

Before he could say anything Julia plunged on, explaining how the insurance business had been so bad all year that Mr. Macklin had to tell her he was going to do his own bookkeeping from now on.

The loan officer looked as though he couldn't wait for her to finish.

"Mrs. Stonecypher, I warn you, I'm impervious to the excuses people invent in my business. Just because I've served you with an eviction notice doesn't mean you have to come up with some story about losing your job. No matter what you tell me, I can't change bank policy. You have to be out of here after the first of the year."

Julia stepped back a step, the envelope still unopened in her hand. Was it true? She could only stare at him. "Do you mean—I—does this mean the bank is going to put us out of our home? But —but you can't do that! Not at *Christmas!*"

He frowned. "I don't seem to be getting through

to you, Mrs. Stonecypher. Didn't you hear what I said? It's December, the end of the fiscal quarter."

Before this man made his way to her door, Julia had tried to bury the terrible news about losing her job in the back of her mind, along with the unpaid heating oil bill and the overdue rent. But now as she stared at the eviction paper she'd pulled from the envelope, she was unable to keep up a good front. The paper had a notary's stamp on it, she saw, with real horror. It looked real, businesslike.

Suddenly she felt like sitting down on the snowy ground and just giving up. She didn't think she had the strength to go on. Things just kept piling up, one on top of the other, until she didn't know how much more she could take.

The loan officer was standing with his arms folded over his chest, regarding her with what could only be stony-faced satisfaction.

It was too much.

"What do you mean," Julia burst out, "you're *sorry*?" She stepped toward him. Startled, he backed up against the side of the Cutlass. "It's fine and good for you to talk about people on Makim's Mountain, how they'd better learn to live in the twentieth century. But if that means acting like *you*, we wouldn't want to!"

"Now, control yourself," he said.

"You were in a mighty big hurry," she went on, heedless, "to drive all the way up here so you could deliver your bad news the day before Christmas Eve!"

He looked down his nose at her. "Do we have to keep harping on Christmas?"

"Around here, people think a lot of Christmas!" Julia crumpled up the paper and threw it at him, but the wind caught it and whirled it away. "Why just make it the day before Christmas Eve?" she cried scornfully. "If you'd tried a little harder you might have managed to get here Christmas *Day* to deliver your wonderful present!"

"Better pick it up, Mrs. Stonecypher." He pointed to the paper on the snowy ground. "You've been served whether you like it or not. And that paper says that in spite of Christmas holidays, Easter, a fire, flood, unemployment or whatever other excuse you try to think of, you still have to vacate the Stonecypher homestead by January second."

Before Julia could speak, he turned on his heel and stalked back to his white Cutlass Ciera. He pulled open the door and slid into the driver's seat. When the engine caught he gunned it hard and then spun the automobile away from the Stonecypher mailbox.

By then the red clay of Makim's Mountain Road had frozen hard. There was a visible powder of snow and under it, ice. As the bank officer's car started down the hill it appeared to hit an icy patch, waggling crazily, its rear wheels spinning. Then it started to slide.

Julia wiped away a few tears with the back of her hand as she watched the Cutlass zigzag toward the curve. Being mountain born, she had long ago learned how to drive on frozen dirt roads.

One of the things you *didn't* do was try to take a skidding car out of a slide by hitting the brakes.

He drove the car just the way he acted, she thought, as the Cutlass slid almost ninety degrees, righted itself, and went forward. He probably made a lot of money being a banker; he certainly showed plain enough what he thought of folks who were poor.

What, she suddenly wondered, was she going to tell her children about all this? It was terrifying for *anybody* to be without a home; she hated to think how Deenie and Emily Rose would take it. They'd been through enough since Jim's death. Now this.

She was at a loss as to what to do. She put one hand on the icy metal of the mailbox, bracing herself to go inside and not let the turmoil of her feelings show in front of her children. *I will get through this Christmas,* she vowed silently. *Not only that, but I'll make it as good as I can for all of us.*

They were brave words. Inside she was feeling like one of the mountain pines clinging to the snow-covered ground around her, about to be uprooted, yanked from the familiar earth. She was not so sure she and her little girls could survive anywhere else.

She turned to go back to the house. As she did so she heard the noise of the Cutlass in a long, slow skid on the road just below.

Julia whirled, her heart in her mouth. He was still in sight; she saw the car head for the road's left side. The Cutlass plowed, nose down, into the deep ditch beyond. There was a loud bang and the sound of breaking glass.

The windshield, she thought wildly. Unless he was the luckiest man on earth, the loan officer was hurt. The Cutlass came to a stop on its side, its wheels spinning.

A second later she started at a run down the driveway.

Two

IT SEEMED THE CRASH OF THE CUTLASS landing in the ditch was loud enough to be heard all the way down to the Makim's Mountain bridge. Probably even as far as Mrs. Dixon's house on the other side.

The noise had drawn Deenie and Emily Rose. They raced across the front yard as Julia jerked open the door on the driver's side.

"Girls, stay back," she yelled, not knowing what she'd find. But, wide-eyed, they squeezed through the door of the Cutlass anyway. Julia bent over the loan officer, who was slumped against the steering wheel.

"He's dead," Dennie screamed. "Oh, Mommy, he's *dead*!"

Julia knew only too well what put that note of terror in her daughter's voice. It *would* have to be another accident, almost on the same spot, she thought. Her own heart was going like a triphammer.

"He isn't dead—now stop screaming. Hush," she told Emily Rose, who was wailing in sympathy. "If you girls will stop making so much noise, you can see he's trying to say something."

"My head," the bank officer groaned.

Blood was pouring down the side of his face. And the windshield, made of safety glass, was smashed in a million beadlike pieces.

"Deenie, keep Emily Rose out of my way," Julia ordered. "Now do as I tell you! I've got to get him out of here." There was always the danger of fire, she remembered, as she tugged at him with all her strength. It was important to hurry. The loan officer suddenly seemed to realize what she was trying to do, for he abruptly lurched sidewise out of the driver's seat, then half fell on her, nearly sending her to her knees in the road.

"My glasses," he said thickly.

"I've got them, Mamma!" Emily Rose wriggled under her sister's arm and grabbed them from the front seat. "Look, I can carry them!"

"No you can't," Deenie said, reaching for them. "They're broken. You'll lose the pieces."

"Girls!" Julia had managed to get her feet under her, but only just barely; it took all her strength to hold him up. On top of that, she was so full of adrenaline she was quivering. "Deenie, if you want to help," she panted, "go hold the front door open. Emily, stick close to me, and for goodness sake, do what I say!"

Her youngest daughter, holding the broken eyeglasses in both hands, trailed them as Julia staggered with the injured man up the driveway. She was trying to tell herself that he couldn't be too badly hurt; at least he could walk. From the way he had acted a few moments ago, practically accusing her of lying, it was hard to feel a whole lot of sympathy.

He stumbled again. Julia pulled his arm across her shoulders to hold him up. Why did something like this have to happen right now? she wondered. She had so many things left to do and no time for something like this! If Santa Claus was going to visit the Stonecypher house she had to hurry up and deliver her Christmas cakes and collect her money. And after that, pick up Deenie's bicycle at Ace Hardware and Emily Rose's precious Barbie doll at Ewing's Variety Store. But now, of course, she couldn't do any of that until she got Mr. Gregory Harding of the Dalton Bank and Trust to the doctor.

He suddenly lurched to a stop. "Whuzzis," he mumbled, looking around him. "Where'm I?"

"At our front steps," Julia told him. "You had an accident with your car, you ran off the road."

He was still bleeding. His white shirt and the front of his overcoat were spattered with red. So, she could see when his coat fell open, was his business suit. For a moment Julia's knees buckled. Please don't let him be badly hurt, she prayed. That would mean calling the ambulance from Dalton. And that could take hours.

"You've got to help me get you inside." She hauled him up so she could speak right into his

ear. "Listen, sir—Mr. Harding—do you understand?"

"Hurry, Mommy," Deenie called from the porch.
"It's snowing hard."

She didn't need to be reminded. "Can you hear
me?" Julia persisted more loudly. "I need to drive
you into Raeburn Gap to the doctor. But first I
need to get you up the steps and into the house."

"Telephone's ringing," Emily Rose shrieked.
She darted up the steps and past her sister.

Deenie looked outraged. *"Mother,* you know
Emily Rose is too little to answer the telephone,
she gets things all mixed up!"

Julia had just managed to get the loan officer to
the top of the steps. "Deenie, hold that door open!
If you go inside and leave me out here . . ." Out of
breath, Julia couldn't finish the rest of her threat.

It didn't matter. Inside, the telephone had
stopped ringing. Julia heard her youngest daughter answering and knew if it *was* Mrs. Dixon on
the other side of the river, the old lady was getting
some of Emily Rose's best three-year-old descrip-
tions of what had happened.

Once inside, Gregory Harding headed for the
living room couch. "Have to," he mumbled, "sit
down."

Julia hauled him back. They were leaving
tracks of snow and blood across the floor. She
pushed him toward what had once been Grandfather Stonecypher's downstairs bedroom. "In
here," she told him.

As soon as he saw the big, Lincoln-style bed, the
loan officer lurched toward it. He hardly gave Julia

time enough to pull off his coat before he fell on it with a crash and then lay still.

Well, *that* didn't take long, she thought, winded. He's out like a light.

Deenie went around to stand at the foot of the bed. "Mother," she said, resigned, "he's dead."

Julia's frayed nerves snapped. "Stop saying that! He's not dead, he's just—" She leaned forward, her hand on the old-fashioned headboard, to peer at him. "He's just passed out," she said, relieved.

Julia had to admit that the man on the bed hardly resembled the arrogant, well-dressed banker who had stepped out of his car into her driveway. Melting snow was reducing his gabardine suit to flabby wrinkles. The front of his jacket, his tie, and the white shirt were blood-spattered, and his chiseled features were unnaturally pale. Even his fine, silky blond hair was matted and sticky. She hated to think what she'd find under all that dried blood.

She abruptly sat down on the side of the bed, feeling her legs would no longer hold her up. She supposed she should get some water and try to see how injured he was, but she was still shaking. Her arm hurt where he had gripped it. And she just plain needed to catch her breath. She was not in such good shape herself.

Don't panic, she told herself, he's made it this far. He's probably too mean and hardhearted to have sustained any major damage. Leaning over, she loosened his tie and pulled it away. He looked more attractive unconscious. At least his lips weren't so tightly clamped together. Without his glasses he had really extraordinary eyelashes—the kind that were long and dark and curled at the tips. The kind any woman would kill for.

Perhaps, Julia thought, somewhat guiltily, he had a concussion. A fractured skull? She remembered she'd read somewhere that being unconscious too long after a head injury wasn't an encouraging sign.

Emily Rose burst into the room, still carrying the gold-rimmed glasses in one fist. "Telephone, Mamma," she shrieked. "Go talk on it!"

Julia sighed. "Thank you, dear." She took the eyeglasses and put them on the night table beside the bed. They were broken. One lens had a large, diagonal crack in it. "Emily Rose, don't climb on the footboard of Grandpa's bed, please, you'll break it. Deenie, you get down, too. And," she said, giving them both warning looks, "don't either of you touch him, do you hear?"

In the kitchen, Julia lifted the telephone receiver to find Mrs. Dixon's voice talking as though her youngest daughter were still on the line. "Dorothy, it's me, Julia Stonecypher," Julia broke in. The excited voice in the receiver rose even higher. "Yes, it's true, a— a man in a car had an accident coming down the road toward the bridge." She wasn't going to tell Dorothy Dixon the man in her downstairs bedroom was the Dalton bank loan officer, and that she was finally going to lose Grandfather Stonecypher's house; she didn't want the whole town of Raeburn Gap to know about it any sooner than they had to.

"I don't care what Emily Rose told you, he's *not* dead," Julia said, more calmly than she felt. "His car ran off the road and landed in the ditch just below my house. Fortunately he wasn't going very fast. Dorothy, I'm in a hurry," she apologized, "you'll have to excuse me, but I have to get the girls dressed and the car loaded so I can deliver my Christmas cakes and take this man into town to the doctor."

Dorothy's voice rose another decibel. "Julia, that's why I'm calling you! I couldn't make little Emily Rose understand what I wanted her to tell you. The radio says we're going to have a big storm, almost a foot of snow. They don't say blizzard, but that's what they mean. And the highway department's just closed the bridge! Julia?" her neighbor cried, "are you there?"

Julia was there, but not for long. There'd been a frazzled burst of loud static in her ear at Dorothy Dixon's last words. Then the telephone receiver went dead in her hand.

As he came up out of the deep black fog that had held him, Gregory Harding was aware of a terrible pounding pain in his head. He lay very still, so as not to make it hurt any worse than it did, and after a few moments he allowed his eyes to roam the room with cautious curiosity.

Where the devil was he, anyway?

An old-fashioned tulip-shaped glass lighting fixture hung from the ceiling directly over him. He could make out a spindle-backed rocker pulled up on his right. On the opposite side of the room was a window with frilly white curtains. Beyond the window glass the sky was gray with falling snow. It filled the room with a silvery, winter light.

He didn't think he was in the hospital; the bed was too comfortable for that. The deep softness surrounded him like a warm nest—a particularly nice place, actually, to be on a snowy winter day. He could see, just below his chin, an old-fashioned patchwork quilt stretching away toward the end of the bed.

Greg suddenly had a mental picture of his mother standing over him, saying, *Now, you put down that picture book and the rest of your toys and just rest your eyes, darling, and I'll bring you a nice cup of tea with honey and lemon in it that will knock out that bad old fever in no time.*

He hadn't remembered what it was like to be sick in bed, feeling so warm and secure, in a long time.

On the other hand, it wasn't too hard to gather that something wasn't quite right. In spite of the comfort and warmth surrounding him, he had a distinct sensation of something gone wrong. He couldn't quite put his finger on it.

Mother?

He didn't think she was there. From what he could tell at that moment, he wasn't a four-year-old but an adult. The body under the brightly colored quilt, for instance, felt definitely like an adult's because it was muscular and somewhat hairy. And from the feel of it, he was wearing a shirt and tie, and a more-than-somewhat-soggy business suit.

All right, so he wasn't a kid sick in bed with a cold, he thought irritably. But where was he? And how had he gotten there? His brain wasn't working at all.

He gradually became aware of voices talking somewhere. Light, airy voices. Then there was a thump on the bed beside him, and something warm and breathing pressed against his side.

Confound it, his head hurt! When he lifted his hand his fingers stuck unpleasantly to his hair. Right in that spot—no, in several spots on his scalp—was where it hurt most. In addition, something was pressing on his arm. Not an unbearable pressure, but there.

It moved slightly. "Squirmed" would be a better word; the weight was warm and it wriggled, like a small body.

"Daaa-dy," it breathed.

Greg carefully slid his eyes to one side. He saw an out-of-focus but plainly ethereal face surrounded by a halo of golden curls. He could assume that a bare two inches beyond his nose there was a cherub with enormous blue eyes that stared at him unwaveringly.

He could see, he found when he squinted painfully, that behind the first cherub stood a somewhat larger version, regarding him just as raptly. The two were so concentrated on him they looked as though they were about to burst into heavenly song.

Ridiculous, he thought. He was hallucinating.

Greg closed his eyes. But when he opened them again, they were still there. It was strange: He had the odd thought that he had never pictured heaven as a place where one woke up in a soft, giant bed, covered by an old-fashioned quilt, surrounded by junior-sized angels.

Angels? But that meant—he was dead!

Three

THE THOUGHT RIPPED THROUGH GREGORY Harding with all the momentum of a runaway freight train.

Dead!

He was dead, he told himself, stunned. Somehow he'd died, and he couldn't remember a thing about how it had happened. He was trying to cope with the implications of this appalling reality when the cherub leaning on his arm opened rosy lips and breathed again, "Daaa-dy."

"Emily, he hears you," the other angel said. "He moved his eyes, can't you see? Now he's looking at you." This angel surveyed Greg kindly but analytically. "Maybe he's just hurt too bad to talk."

He was finding he couldn't see much of anything without his glasses. But "Daddy," the smallest one had said. So he wasn't dead, he thought, a little surprised to find himself so relieved.

And these were not budget-sized angels but little girls, he thought as he struggled to focus his eyes on them.

All right, he was alive. That made sense—he could hardly be dead the way he felt, with his head pounding like it was going to break in half. What *was* odd was that according to the evidence he was seeing, he was the father of two little daughters.

That was hardly wonderful; he distinctly remembered he was not the marrying kind. From what he'd seen of his friends' marriages, it was a confused and inevitably unhappy estate, and he had tried to avoid it like the plague. On the other hand, there was no denying the children were *there*.

He surveyed them surreptitiously out of one eye.

Little girls. Daughters, not even boys. Still, he had to admit they were above average in looks. No wonder he had mistaken them for angels.

Common politeness, if nothing else, demanded he not just lie there, letting them wonder how he was. "Hello," Greg Harding croaked.

He knew instantly that he'd made a mistake. The moment he'd opened his mouth a giant pain laced through his head, making him unable to do much of anything but lie there, waiting for it to go away.

At about the time the terrible pain halved his skull, the angelic little voices began to fade. He realized he was losing consciousness again. He could hear them, his daughters, talking, sliding into the distance. With a groan Greg Harding let himself drop back down into blessed, numbing blackness.

Julia filled a pan full of hot water at the kitchen sink and laid a clean washcloth in it. With luck, they could get rid of the bank officer in a few hours. Telephone lines on Makim's Mountain seldom went down for more than that; most times the trouble was somewhere else, usually on the main trunks that went south to Dalton.

She wasn't so sure about the bridge. Still, the last time freezing rain had layered the old iron girders with tons of glistening ice, the county highway department had waited a day for a thaw and, when it didn't come, they'd sent a crew out on the shaky structure to salt it down. Within a few hours, the ice had melted and the bridge was opened.

They're going to do something of the sort this time, she told herself hopefully. If they'd only do it in the next few hours. She not only had to get their accident victim to a doctor in Raeburn Gap, she had to get to town to deliver her special-order pound cakes and collect her money.

This Christmas Julia had wished in vain for just enough cash to get Santa's gifts a little bit earlier, rather than at the last minute. Particularly since Deenie's insistence on believing in Santa Claus had turned into such a touchy subject. But the money just hadn't been there.

If there was a right age for Santa Claus, she couldn't help thinking, Emily Rose, who had just turned three, seemed perfect for it. At that age everything was wonderfully uncomplicated. Emily loved Santa, clapping her hands and squealing every time she saw him on television. But things were different with Deenie, and it worried her. In the fourth grade, most kids prided themselves on being cynical Santa *non*believers. This year, they had teased Deenie unmercifully about it.

Holding the pan of water in one hand, Julia rummaged in the hall closet for some shirts that were waiting to be taken to the church charity clothing box.

Nadina Elizabeth, named for her two grandmothers, was her dreamy, otherworldly child. When Jim died, Deenie refused to accept it; for a long time after the accident she wouldn't believe he was dead. *My daddy's in the hospital,* she'd tell anyone who'd listen. *And in a little while he's coming home.*

Well, Deenie wasn't the only one who hadn't wanted to let the memory of her father fade. Julia, too, had found it hard to part with the loving ghost of Jim Stonecypher. For months after he'd gone, she'd sobbed late into the night, wanting him so much it seemed she would literally weep her heart out. Jim knew how she was; he'd told her so many times, *Lord, Julia, you never give up. Just once, you ought to learn how to let go.*

Now Deenie and Emily Rose were two years older, and sometimes it seemed to Julia none of them would ever fully recover from the terrible hole Jim's death had left in their lives.

She pulled a blue plaid shirt out of the pile. Her hand hesitated over the jeans. The bank officer's clothes were wet. She supposed she should get them off him before he caught pneumonia. She probably couldn't put his expensive suit in the dryer, but she could hang it up in the laundry room, where it was warm. If they were extra lucky and the bridge opened before dark, there was a chance his own clothes would be dry by then.

There was a time when just the sight of Jim's clothes pierced her like a sword. There was something so familiar in the soft flannel fabric, something so agonizing in the cuffs that had wrapped around his strong wrists, the collar that had encircled his neck. It sounded idiotic, but seeing Jim's clothes without his fine strong body in them had been like seeing a ghost that stayed too long to haunt her. They were still part of him, lying clean and neatly stacked in the closet.

She pushed the shirts back into their pile. This year she had put Jim's things in a box to take to the clothing collection at church. Where someone else, who needed good clothes to work in, could use them.

Julia sorted through the jeans. The bank officer would need pants when he got out of bed. At worst, she was thinking, they would have him overnight—hopefully not that long. She put Dorothy Dixon's words about the forecast blizzard resolutely out of her mind.

When Julia came into the bedroom, both girls were hanging on the high walnut footboard, staring at the man under the quilt.

"He woke up," Deenie told her. "He woke up and saw us, and he said hello. He looked straight at us. Oh, Mamma, he's so nice! Wouldn't it be wonderful if we had him for our stranger for Christmas? You know, the one we always put the chair at the table for on Christmas Eve?"

Julia had forgotten her children had no idea who this man was. That, she knew suddenly, was sheer luck. If only she could think of some way to keep them from finding out.

"That's what the story's about," her oldest child was saying. "That people keep a place ready for the Christmas stranger."

Julia's patience was thin. "Deenie, please don't go making up Christmas stories when I have just about as much as I can handle right now!" She dragged a spool-backed chair to the bed and put the pan of hot water down on it. Then she laid the clean shirt and jeans on the quilt.

She could see it didn't pay to snap at her daughters; they were both looking at her now with big, wounded eyes.

"All right," Julia said, more softly, "you can both help me. Deenie, you go get a bottle of shampoo so I can clean his hair and see how badly he's hurt."

"It's *not* a made-up story, Mother!" Deenie leaned against her arm. "There's always a chair left at the table at Christmastime for the stranger. Grandma and Grandpa Stonecypher always left a chair—so did Granny Makim. Sometimes even at Thanksgiving."

Julia lifted his arm to ease off his bloodstained shirt. "Nadina Elizabeth, the empty chair we leave at the table at Christmastime is an old custom, so old I can't remember who started it—probably our great-great-grandfolks who settled these mountains. But it's a symbol of"—she managed to shove the loan officer's hand into the sleeve of the clean shirt with some difficulty—"any of the world's people who need a roof over their heads at Christmas. Not just any fool who happens to smash up his car in front of your house."

She found she had to prop the loan officer against her to get the shirt pulled down in back. As she did so, she was suddenly sharply conscious of the feel of his warm, bare skin through her clothes. It caught her by surprise, and it bothered her more than she would have expected, to find him so heavy and muscular in her arms. She eased him back to the bed, careful of his head, and jerked the quilt over him.

"Now, with luck," she said, trying to sound casual, "we can get Mr.—we can get this man out of here before dark. That is, if the highway department will get the bridge open."

Emily Rose had climbed up on the bed. "Daddy," she murmured, reaching out to pat his cheek.

"He's *not* your daddy!" Julia took her by the arm and pulled her down. "Now you girls listen to me. He's probably got a wife and children of his own, back wherever he comes from. Don't," she said, giving Emily's bottom a pat, "call him 'Daddy' anymore, do you hear?"

"The bridge is closed?" Deenie gave a little bounce on the footboard, shaking the bed. "Mamma, didn't I *tell* you? We do have the Christmas stranger!" She paused to watch Julia strip off the man's shoes and trousers under the cover of the quilt. "Oh, Mother," she whispered urgently, "we can keep him for Christmas, can't we?"

Julia straightened, flushed, the bank officer's trousers in her hand. This business was getting out of hand. She didn't know what had gotten into her children.

"Keep him? The man's had an accident on the road, he's not some sort of Christmas . . . *present.* He's just some stranger who was driving by." That was not a complete lie, she told herself; as far as she knew, the loan officer *was* a stranger. "If the telephone comes back on I'm going to call the sheriff's department. And the doctor. We've got to get him out of here somehow."

She moved the basin of water closer to the bed and took the warm washcloth and began to soak the dried blood from his hair. Under her fingers, she could feel several gashes in his scalp and knew they accounted for most of the bleeding. It didn't look like there was anything more, except, of course, the possibility that he had a concussion.

Sighing loudly, Deenie went to fetch the shampoo.

I wish you'd wake up, Julia told her patient silently, *you're making me nervous. And my children are beginning to make some sort of Christmas myth out of you that you don't deserve.*

She pushed Grandmother Stonecypher's handmade star quilt to one side to keep from wetting it, then rinsed his hair. Naked except for his revealing white cotton jockey shorts, the man on the bed lay very still.

Julia looked down at the smooth, muscled expanse of his chest and shoulders, the flat plane of his belly. He was a good-looking man, she had to admit, and very virile. There was an impressive male bulge under his underwear.

She bit her lip, thinking it would have probably been a good idea to send the girls from the room while she practically stripped him. On the other hand, making a big thing over a man's body would only make her girls think there was some forbidden mystery there.

Forbidden mystery?

Julia held the forgotten washcloth in her hand as she stared down at him. She didn't know why she'd thought of those particular words, except that the man's body was, well, *mysterious.* And amazingly sexy. He was surprisingly *golden*—the light sprinkle of hair on his chest had gold glints in it, as did the hair on his wrists and arms. Even his longish blond hair slid silkily through her fingers as she washed it. Goodness, Julia thought, it had been so long since they'd had a man in the house; somehow it was nice just looking at him. And more than that. Where she touched him her fingers seemed to grow more than usually tingly and warm.

Emily Rose propped her elbows on the bed. "Daddy," she murmured.

Deenie came back with the shampoo. "Without his clothes on," she said, regarding the man on the bed with undisguised interest, "he *does* look a lot like Daddy."

That did it. Julia poured some shampoo into her hand and lathered his hair briskly. The bank officer wasn't at all like Jim Stonecypher, who had been a big, powerful man with a white flashing grin and reckless black eyes. He would dare anything, ride anything—horses or motorcycles—and he was a wonderful lover.

In contrast, the man stretched out on Grandpa Stonecypher's bed had a lean, graceful body built like a swimmer or a tennis player. He was taller than Jim, even though Jim, too, had been well over six feet. And, Julia remembered, the loan officer was heavier than he looked; she had a sore arm that would testify to that. She rinsed the shampoo out of his hair, careful of the cuts on his scalp.

"That's it, girls," she told them. "Now, both of you go into the kitchen and see what you can do to help me get the rest of my Christmas cakes wrapped. I'll be with you as soon as I pick up in here."

Deenie didn't move. "Mamma, I can sit in here and watch him?" she pleaded. "He's been hurt, he needs somebody to watch him until he wakes up again, doesn't he?"

"Daddy," Emily Rose said, trying to climb back up on the bed.

"Stop this." Julia pulled her down by the back of her shirt. "You, too, Deenie."

She shooed them to the door and into the hallway in the direction of the kitchen in spite of their protests. When she came back, she stood looking down at Gregory Harding. If she could just get him back on his feet, she was tempted to walk him the four miles herself down Makim's Mountain to the bridge. She would send him across, no matter what condition the bridge was in. Or *he* was in.

Bending over him, she studied that good-looking, patrician face. Even unconscious he looked smug. He was not the sort of man she would ever be interested in. She didn't like people who were cold-blooded and ruthless.

She bent to pick up his wet clothes from the floor. Well, he wasn't her responsibility, thank goodness. She couldn't wait to get rid of him.

Greg opened his eyes a second time. As the blackness receded he saw it was the same room, even though the light had grown dimmer. He needed his glasses; he was tired of looking at things through a confounded blur.

But wait a minute! The nerve endings behind his eyes registered alarm. Another vision, just as vague as the ones before, was now in the room with him.

Blast it, it would help a lot if he could remember who he was. And where he was.

Greg knew he had a devil of a bump on his head, and he supposed his memory would come to him eventually. But in the meantime, not being able to remember was exasperating. Especially since what he could see of this new arrival told him she was attractive in a sweet, slightly mussed, totally natural-looking way. Her dark hair was piled at the top of her head and spilled down in back over a long, graceful neck. Her face was a pale oval, shadowed with darkly luminous eyes. Her figure, what he could see of it under a bag lady's sweater and worn jeans, was tall, leggy, delightful. Someone—his uncle?—had told him about her.

Greg knotted his brows. Immediately this sent a sharp pain through his skull. *Better not to think,* he told himself.

He couldn't help it, he had to. The two little girls were his, weren't they? Hadn't they called him "Daddy"?

He was aware that he was involved in some sort of complicated situation. Because that meant that she, then, was obviously—

He cleared his throat to get her attention, dreading what he'd hear. "You must be my wife," he said hoarsely.

"Your *wife*?" The vision moved over him, eyes looking right at him. "Good heavens, what are you talking about?"

He took a deep breath. Looking up into those dazzling dark eyes had a dizzying effect on him. "I don't know." Greg felt his head and winced. "I've been hurt somehow, haven't I?"

"You mean you don't remember anything?" He saw her hesitate. "You had an accident, your car ran off the road. I suppose you don't remember that, either?"

He'd had an accident. The only reassuring thing seemed to be that he was still in one piece.

"I've got two daughters?" He wasn't ready to admit to anything yet.

She kept staring at him. He heard her murmur, "I just don't believe it." She bent over him, dark eyes searching his face. "You mean you really don't know who you are?"

He wanted to hang onto consciousness this time and not fade away just when he was learning something. He wanted to know more about this woman, and the little girls. And how he had managed to get into something like this.

"I don't remember a thing," he admitted. "Listen, what about the car?" He knew he had a car, a business car; it belonged to the bank. If anything happened to it, he was liable.

Unfortunately, the overwhelming darkness was returning. In spite of everything, Greg knew he was slipping away.

She had taken his hand. "Your eyes are glazing over again," he heard her say. "Oh, please, can't you stay awake long enough for me to ask you a few questions?"

Her hand felt very soothing and soft. "It's all right," he managed to say. "Not to worry, it's probably just a—a concussion."

He heard her gasp. At that point Greg lost track of what he was saying. Then he felt his eyes close.

Julia still held his hand. It couldn't be true. She couldn't believe this man really didn't know where he was or *who* he was. He thought Deenie and Emily Rose were his daughters, and that she was his wife!

He must have lost his memory when he hit the windshield. Maybe he had . . . *amnesia.*

Julia didn't know much about amnesia herself, but in Raeburn Gap nearly everybody watched daytime television, and amnesia happened on soap operas all the time. From what Julia had heard, amnesia victims could have their condition for months, or even *years*.

Her mind was whirling. It was difficult to wish him anything really bad, even someone who was going to evict her and her family. But she'd just had a thought. If only the loan officer's memory would stay lost for a while! Say, at least until she got him out of her house.

In the next breath Julia told herself that what she was thinking was crazy. And wicked! One had to be a vile sort of person to take advantage of an injured man, unless, of course, he was the sort who would do the same thing to you.

Holding his trousers, she emptied his pockets of keys and some change. When she came to his English leather wallet she stopped to glance at him furtively. She breathed a sigh of relief when she saw his eyes were still closed.

You ought to be ashamed of yourself, Julia Stonecypher, her inner voice spoke up, *picking an unconscious man's pockets!*

I just don't want him to wake up, find his wallet, and know who he is, Julia defended herself.

She flipped open the wallet. Her mouth dropped open when she saw how much money there was. It looked like more than two or three hundred dollars, plus several credit cards and a membership in something called a Bath and Racket Club. So he *was* a tennis player. She could just see him, lean and blond and dressed all in white, bounding around the tennis courts in some expensive country club.

His driver's license gave his full name as Gregory Ailsworth Harding. There were auto insurance and hospital insurance cards, even a card to get a free frozen yogurt after it was punched the tenth time.

Julia's lip curled. It was easy to think of him as someone who'd never struggled very hard. Someone named Gregory Ailsworth Harding who had been raised in a privileged world to think there was no real reason poor people couldn't pay their rent.

If, she suddenly promised herself, he wakes up and remembers who he is, I'll give him back his wallet and driver's license and all his identification. I don't mean to keep it, anyway, but I am going to protect my girls. I want to make this the best Christmas I can, since it may be the last one we'll have in Grandpa Stonecypher's house.

There was certainly no part in it for this man, who could spoil everything.

She shoved the wallet down deep in her cardigan pocket. Then, moving quietly, she turned off the light and went out.

From under half-closed eyes, Gregory Harding had seen the woman take his wallet out of his trousers. It had taken him a few groggy minutes to figure out what she was doing.

Well, that's human nature for you, he thought, unsurprised. Especially up here in the mountains where these people were a law unto themselves.

The theft instantly eliminated any positive feelings he might have had about the little girls and this singularly innocent-looking woman who, he now knew, was definitely *not* his wife.

Because lying there, watching her commit her act of thievery, Gregory Harding had suddenly remembered who he was and where he was. At the moment he was in someone's bed in the Stonecypher house on Makim's Mountain. He'd lost control of his car in a snowstorm and clumsily run it into a ditch.

And, he reminded himself, the woman was a thief and a deadbeat. He knew she cheated on her rent. Now he'd just seen her lift his wallet.

Greg could admit that he had no one but himself to blame. Making this trip to the mountains had been, he could see now, poorly thought out. This was all he needed, to get stuck up in the hills in bad weather, with a wrecked car. The bank's Cutlass was probably still in the ditch at the front of the house.

He winced as he touched the cuts on his head. He'd smacked the windshield. From the blurriness of his vision, even without his glasses, he was pretty sure he had at least a slight concussion.

His *glasses.* He really needed his eyeglasses—he was both myopic and astigmatic, blind as a bat without them. Maybe, he thought with a burst of peevishness, she'd pinched his glasses, too.

He really couldn't understand what her game was. Oh, the Widow Stonecypher was great on the eyes if you liked them tall and willowy, with a sort of natural, unspoiled beauty. But she had revealed her nasty disposition quickly enough when he tried to explain the legal facts of delinquent rent. Quite a vicious little temper, too. She'd actually thrown the eviction paper back at him.

Greg hauled himself up on his elbow, wincing. If she had a confederate maybe she planned to rob him, knock him in the head, and dump his body in the nearest creek. That wasn't too damned far-fetched, the way crime was going these days.

He was thinking hard, in spite of his hurting head, and that was progress. He wasn't so groggy now; he was actually fairly alert. He was going to need his wits about him. He had to get out of bed, do a little investigating, and find out what was really going on.

Except, he discovered when he threw back the quilt, someone had taken his pants.

Four

THE SNOWSTORM WAS FAST COVERING THE north Georgia hills. Standing on the back porch, Julia could just make out the boundaries of the pasture in back of the house and, beyond it, the old Cherokee burying ground along Black Kettle Creek. On the slopes of Makim's Mountain snow coated the pine trees like cake frosting, bending their branches almost to the ground. And underneath, the rough boulders and scrub of the mountainside were already transformed by a carpet of white.

Somewhere in all that white-speckled gray, Julia knew, the sun was setting. It was still getting colder. The back porch thermometer showed the low twenties.

She wasn't worried yet, though, about the storm. The solid old house, built with mountain granite blocks over the original hand-hewn logs of the first Stonecypher cabin was strong enough to withstand almost anything. So, thank goodness, was Jim's almost-new roof. They had plenty of food. Her pantry was still full from the summer's canning. As for fuel oil . . .

Well, Julia thought ruefully, it was too bad the bank officer wasn't there on the back porch to lecture her about the sins of not paying her bills. But with a little luck, and keeping the thermostat turned down, perhaps they'd scrape by with what was left in the tank.

Once, when she was a child, there had been a record-setting blizzard in the southern Appalachians and it had snowed, almost nonstop, for seventy-two hours. She still remembered the excitement, the dreamlike unreality of being shut off from Raeburn Gap, from the world. It had been days before the county road scrapers, designed for dirt road maintenance, not snow, had cleared the roads, and in all that time Makim's Mountain had been locked in a world of frozen, glistening white. With a houseful of cousins down the road to frolic with, Julia hadn't appreciated the grown-ups' efforts to keep them all warm and fed and the livestock cared for, until years later.

It could happen again, she knew. She was not worrying now about the bank officer lying in Grandpa Stonecypher's bed and how she was going to get him to town, but about two little girls who still believed in Santa Claus. If the bridge stayed closed tomorrow, the used bicycle she'd gotten for Deenie and Emily Rose's Barbie doll would be left in town.

Oh, lord, she hadn't really considered that! It was terrible to think of having Christmas without Santa's gifts. Even during the worst of the Great Depression, nothing like that had ever happened to the Makims, or the Stonecyphers, or any of the mountain families, that Julia could remember.

In hard times, someone always made cornshuck dolls for the girls and whittled pinewood play animals for the boys. For Christmas Day there was at least dried apple pie or sorghum candy. No matter how poor, mountain people always managed Christmas for their children somehow.

What would she do on Christmas morning when the girls woke up and found no gifts under the Christmas tree? Sit both of them down and tell them a blizzard and a bank officer who'd wrecked his car had canceled everything, because *she* hadn't been able to get to town to pick up their toys?

And there really *wasn't* a Santa Claus?

Julia leaned her head against one of the wooden posts of the unfinished back porch. She was freezing. She knew she should go inside, but she had to take a moment to think.

Oh, Jim, if only you hadn't gone off and left me! I need you so much! It was a silent wail of hurt she hadn't given in to for months.

But, oh, how she needed him! Her problems with Deenie, her helplessness before Emily Rose's belief that every man was her missing daddy, all rolled up suddenly into a ball of misery that was as soul-chilling as the wind tearing up the mountain slopes from the valley. After a few minutes standing there, gripping the very wooden post Jim had put up when he started to rebuild the porch, Julia realized her bare hands were turning to ice.

She rubbed them against the wood, feeling the rime and snow frozen to it.

Jim was gone, leaving so much undone, unfinished, and still waiting for him. Like the work on the porch. Like her aching, unfinished love.

Jim is dead, Julia told herself for the thousandth time. She would have to go on alone; that was nothing new. She would have to try to do a good job, just as Jim would have wanted her to. But it was so hard. She still hadn't come up with any idea of how to handle Christmas without Santa's gifts, if that should come to pass.

A burst of childish voices inside the house reminded her of where she was and what she'd been doing when she drifted off: checking the temperature and worrying about the heating oil.

Julia stuck her cold hands under her coat and bent once more to take a look at the thermometer. It had dropped another degree. Then she straightened and started for the back door.

The kitchen smelled of cake waiting to be wrapped. Deenie and Emily Rose were at the pine table that had been used to serve Stonecypher family meals for more than a century, working with aluminum foil and red Christmas ribbon. Or at least Deenie was. Emily Rose was busy unwinding red ribbon from the spool and watching it spill onto the floor in piles of shimmering coils.

"Mother," Deenie said at once, "look what Emily Rose is doing!"

Julia took a deep breath, savoring the warm, happy fragrance of her kitchen. Before their modest savings had run out, Jim's remodeling had centered here, because it was where the family spent most of its time. He had opened up the old brick fireplace, repaired the hearth, and replaced Grandpa's old "ice box"—really a 1950s refrigerator—with a new one and a freezer. But Julia's pride and joy was her modern electric stove and wall-mounted microwave oven. The kitchen was the place she loved, truly the heart of the house.

She sat down at the table and her youngest daughter, face full of mischief, planted her elbows in the midst of several pecan-covered cakes and leaned toward her lovingly. "Christmas, Mommy," she shouted. "I help!"

Deenie gave a cry of sisterly indignation. "Mother, will you please just *look* what she's done? Emily Rose has torn all the aluminum foil off the cakes I just did. She ruins everything!"

Julia lifted Emily Rose from the scene of destruction and dropped her back in her high chair. "She's only trying to help, Deenie." Tempted, she scooped up a pinch of one of the more battered cakes and popped it into her mouth. The rich, buttery flavor melted against her tongue. "Remember Christmas," she said, touching her daughter's cheek with the back of her hand. "Goodwill to all mankind, hmmm? Including your baby sister?"

She broke off another piece of pecan cake. It was almost suppertime, but eating just a crumb of

Stonecypher pound cake was impossible; it was too good.

The Stonecypher recipe had come into being, according to Jim's mother, in the early part of the last century, when Lucius Stonecypher, a veteran of the Delaware regiment in the Revolutionary War, had received land in the north Georgia mountains from Congress for his services. When he settled on the mountain, Lucius took as his bride a local part-Cherokee belle who, thanks to her marriage, was spared the terrible Trail of Tears some years later when the Cherokees were forcibly driven off their lands under Andrew Jackson.

The recipe for pound cake had been Lucius Stonecypher's bride's, brought to her marriage with her other household goods. It was made with ingredients measured according to the times: a pound of butter, a pound of flour, a pound of sugar. All sorts of nuts, depending upon what one could gather in the woods, were in the original recipe, including the wonderful-tasting but hard-to-pick-out hickory nut. Half a century later, Amos Stonecypher's Spanish-American War bride from Florida substituted pecans and bourbon for the brandy and hickory nuts.

Stonecypher pound cake had long been famous at county fairs and church suppers by the time Julia married Jim. It was only during the past two years, when Julia began to bake Stonecypher pound cakes to sell, that she'd tinkered with the ingredients to bring the recipe up-to-date with sour cream, bought at the Raeburn Gap super-market, for extra richness and moisture.

During the Thanksgiving and Christmas holi-days, she had almost too many orders to fill, Julia thought, viewing the cakes that covered the big wooden table, the flat surfaces of the kitchen cabi-nets, and even the windowsills. If the storm kept them on Makim's Mountain tomorrow, she hated to think how much money she would lose. Not only what she would have earned, but also the cost of the ingredients that had taken the rest of what she'd had in the bank.

"Mother." Deenie's small hand slipped over hers softly as she looked up into Julia's face. "You're worrying again."

"Am I?" For once, Julia couldn't manage a smile. She pulled a roll of red Christmas ribbon away from Emily Rose, who had unwound several more yards of it.

"Mommy, I help *wrap,*" her youngest protested.

"Only when you learn to tie a bow," Julia told her. "Otherwise you have to leave this to Deenie and me. Girls, listen." Two pairs of eyes, one pair china blue, the other brown like her own behind gold-rimmed eyeglasses, turned to her. "What if it keeps on snowing?" she said carefully. "You know, not just a storm, but a real blizzard like the ones up north that we see on television." While her children sat silently, Julia took a deep breath and went on, "What I'm trying to say is there might be so much snow Santa can't get through to us this Christmas."

"Santa's comin'," Emily Rose shouted. "And Rudolph Rendose Rain Ear with him! And Crosby Snowman!"

Deenie looked relieved. "Oh, Mother, you don't have to worry about *that*," she chided wisely. "Everybody knows Santa's reindeer fly through the air. They won't care at all about the bridge being closed." She reached in front of Julia for another loaf cake to wrap. "Besides, we know everything's going to be all right. We have a Christmas stranger who's come to stay with us. Just like they did in the old days."

Julia stared at her child, unable, for a long moment, to think of anything to say. Christmas stranger, indeed! How could she convince her daughters the man in Grandpa Stonecypher's bed hardly intended anything *good* for them?

"Deenie, the man who had a wreck in front of the house has nothing to do with our Christmas," she said. "If the bridge clears up tomorrow we're going to take him into town to the doctor. He doesn't belong with us, he has family in Dalton." She hesitated. "Or somewhere."

Her daughter looked forbearing. "But Mother, that's why you said people looked for the Christmas stranger. You remember—somebody who's lost and needs a roof over his head?"

"Well, I didn't mean him." Julia smoothed out the red satin ribbon on her pound cake where she'd yanked it too tight. "Deenie, he has *nothing* to do with Christmas. On the contrary, he—" She stared at her children in frustration. "Look, let's just say I hope he's long gone by tomorrow!"

"So do I."

Julia whirled in her chair.

The loan officer was standing in the kitchen doorway, disheveled and sleepy-eyed, modestly wrapped from the waist down in Grandma Stonecypher's star pattern quilt. She couldn't stop her eyes from traveling down his well-muscled form. Despite herself, she was drawn to him. He was wearing Jim's old blue plaid shirt Julia had struggled to put on him; his broad shoulders stretched the material tight. At the sight, her heart gave an unwilling lurch.

"Just where," he demanded, "are my pants?"

"Daddy," Emily Rose breathed, slipping down from her chair.

Julia caught her just in time. "I—I was just coming to see how you were." Be careful, she reminded herself; there was no telling what this man would say in front of the girls.

He swayed a little. "As a matter of fact, I seem to be missing not only my pants but my wallet." He paused significantly. "I don't suppose you'd know anything about that?"

Julia flushed. The wallet was still a bulge in her cardigan pocket. Carefully, she put her hand over it. If he still didn't remember who he was—or why he'd come—she certainly wasn't going to give it back to him.

She said quickly, "I—ah, I've been so busy I haven't had time to keep track of everything." She was growing even more flustered under that accusing stare. "I didn't know if you were hurt. I mean, I knew you were hurt, I could see you were *bleeding*. But I had to get you out of those clothes.

They were . . . wet," she ended, her voice trailing off.

"That was very kind of you." He meant just the opposite. "I want to use your telephone, if you don't mind." He blinked, trying to focus his eyes. "That's my car, isn't it, in the ditch in front of the house? I need to call a tow truck."

Deenie jumped up. "The telephone's out," she said eagerly. "You can't call out at all until they get it fixed. But we have—my *daddy* had—a tractor. Mamma can drive it, it's still in the barn. We'll be glad to pull your car out with—"

"Deenie, *hush!*" Julia struggled to hold onto Emily Rose. "The tractor hasn't been used in a long time. I don't even know if there's gas in it."

"Never mind," he said stiffly, "I have a better idea. If you'll give my suit back to me, I'll get dressed and walk back to town myself."

"The bridge is out, too," Deenie told him promptly. "You're going to have to stay here for Christmas. You're our Christmas stranger. Mamma says—"

"You haven't been awake," Julia almost shouted, "to know what's been happening." She pushed Deenie back down in her chair. "But we've had almost six inches of snow since you—since you were hurt. Makim's Mountain bridge is so old and rickety the county closes it down when there's too much snow or ice on it."

An incredulous scowl froze on his face. *"Closes it down?"*

Julia couldn't meet his eyes. She knew she was looking the picture of guilt and hated herself for it.

Dear heaven, how she longed to get rid of this man!

"Yes, they close it with a chain. Then they put barriers up." When he said nothing, she went on. "The bridge has been marked for replacement for years, but every time the funding comes up in the legislature, the summer people on the mountain send petitions to the capital asking that the bridge be designated an historic site. So the bridge never gets torn down to make way for a new one because of the preservationists. And without highway funding, it can't get repaired, either."

She got up, holding a squirming Emily Rose in her arms. "You do remember that you had an accident?" she said, peering at him. "A few minutes—a while back, when you woke up in the other room, you didn't seem to remember who you were."

The bank loan officer had gone perfectly still. The news about the Makim's Mountain bridge had apparently come as a shock. "Remember?" he muttered absently. "Who I am? Why shouldn't I—" He stopped abruptly.

She saw him take a deep breath and look around, his gaze resting briefly on Emily Rose and Deenie, who were watching him adoringly.

"As a matter of fact," he said in a different tone of voice, "I was hoping *you'd* know. Without my wallet I can't even check my driver's license, and I don't seem to have any other identification. I not only don't know who I am, I don't know who *you* are."

Julia put Emily Rose back on her feet. "I'm

Julia Stonecypher, and these are my daughters," she said, gesturing toward her children. "Nadina Elizabeth and Emily Rose."

The only thing she could say for this obnoxious man was that at least the girls liked him; she could hardly keep them away from him. He seemed unusually calm for a man who'd just lost his memory, she thought to herself. *He hasn't lost his memory*, Julia knew in the next instant. He was pretending!

But *why*?

Suddenly, the cold hand of irrational fear clutched at her. Was there something wrong with him? After all, she was alone in the house, she hardly knew him, she'd taken his word when he'd said who he was. He may have been knocked silly from the blow to his head when she'd talked to him in Grandpa Stonecypher's room a little while ago, but she couldn't fathom why he would continue, now, to pretend he couldn't remember. Unless—oh, horrors—he was a psychotic ax murderer or something like that, just pretending to be a banker!

"Daddy!" Emily Rose slipped out of her grasp and threw herself at his legs. Or approximately where they would be under the quilt. "Santa's comin'!" she cried, hugging him enthusiastically.

Julia dragged her away. Up close, she supposed he did look more like an arrogant, unfeeling money-grubber than a psychotic killer. "It's the shirt," she explained reluctantly. "My daughter thinks you're her father because you're wearing his shirt."

His expression was icy. "If you don't mind, I'd like to get my clothes back. I can't stay here." He looked around the kitchen with distaste. "Some-one must be looking for me. I—ah, have family, I'm sure, waiting for me, so I don't want to have you—er, keep me here."

"I'm not keeping you here!" Julia flared at him. "Good heavens, don't you realize the telephone is out, and the bridge is closed? There's nothing I can do about that!"

She turned on her heel and went to the stove. This was a fine way to begin Christmas. If he had to stay there, in her house, for more than just the night, she knew she would end up wanting to strangle him.

She poured water into the electric coffeemaker, keeping her back to him. Just the thought of the bank's loan officer standing in her kitchen in his underwear and her husband's good shirt made her so furious she couldn't bear to look at him. She hadn't heard a word of thanks, either.

After she'd put in the coffee filter, she said in what she hoped was a neutral voice, "You can do what you want, but I don't think you're in any shape to walk down Makim's Mountain to the bridge. It's all of four miles, and the snow's proba-bly waist deep by now where the wind's piled it up."

When she glanced over her shoulder, he was still standing in the doorway in his stocking feet, holding that ridiculous quilt around his hips. She suddenly remembered his shoes were in the downstairs bathroom where she'd put them to dry.

"You might as well sit down," Julia said ungraciously. "You're in my way where you are. I've got supper to fix."

She thought he was going to say something. But when she looked at him he'd gone white as a sheet. Beads of perspiration had popped out on his face. Then, with a lurch, the loan officer hitched up the quilt, staggered across the kitchen, and sat down beside Deenie and Emily Rose.

Julia watched him, openmouthed. "Are you all right?" He certainly didn't look it. "I was just going to fix you some coffee."

He propped his elbow on the table, dragged the quilt over his bare legs, and lowered his tousled blond head to his hand. "Anything," he muttered, wincing. "Yes, coffee. Aspirin, too, if you've got it."

Deenie regarded him with a totally fascinated expression. "Mommy," she said softly, "I don't think the Christmas stranger feels too good."

Julia found herself counting to ten. Then, mouthing a few rude words under her breath, she reached up into the cabinet for the can of coffee and the aspirin bottle.

Greg Harding's head was swimming. Dizziness had come over him so suddenly it had almost taken his legs out from under him in the midst of, he was remembering, some witless conversation with the unsavory Widow Stonecypher. By now he was fairly sure he had a concussion; just a minute before he had started seeing double, a sure sign.

That had brought a momentary attack of nausea; he'd nearly thrown up.

He certainly wasn't in the care of what you'd call intelligent, responsible people. He could be dying of a skull fracture as a result of lack of proper medical attention for all they cared. Maybe that was how she thought she could get out of her eviction. Kill the man who had just served her with the papers.

Around him, the children's reedlike voices swelled and then receded. The kitchen was insufferably hot. He knew he didn't have time to be stranded up here in the mountains; things were in an organizational flux at the bank, and he couldn't take any time off, especially not in the holiday season.

Coffee. It was somewhere.

With an effort, Greg opened his eyes. The angel's baby face was back, huge blue eyes shining. The kid, he remembered with a sinking feeling, who thought he was her daddy. "Don't say it," he muttered. "Just don't say the word."

He fumbled for the cup. He hadn't been able to find his glasses since she took his clothes away. His elbow brushed something and he looked down. *Cake?* The place seemed to be filled with cakes. Hundreds of them. It was bizarre. Two little girls were seated with him at a giant, cake-filled table. He tried to find the third one. There she was, pouring coffee into his cup. Big, dark eyes, black, curling hair, a fascinating mouth, and that figure.

He had to remember that she was the backwoods con artist who'd made off with his clothes.

The standard move to make sure he didn't wander. All his life he'd heard stories about these mountain people—that they were clannish as gypsies, that they had killed each other off in feuds not too many years ago, and that when among them, any civilized person had to watch his back.

The story about the bridge being closed was easy enough to check. As soon as he could get his legs under him he was going to see for himself.

Greg peered at the coffee she'd just put in front of him. God, he needed his glasses! She could drug him and he'd never know. If she could lift his wallet in the bedroom, he wouldn't put anything past her.

Over the clatter he heard her say, "Deenie, I'm going to feed Miss Piggy. It's snowing too hard for you to go out yourself."

He started. What did that mean? He looked around, half expecting to see a pig sitting there at the table. In the next moment the conversation was about someone's 4-H pig that needed to be fed. Because it was snowing, she was going to go out to the barn and do it.

With unsteady hands, Greg lifted his cup. The coffee was delicious, the only satisfying thing he'd found since he'd gotten out of the warm, soft bed. His glasses, his wallet, his pants, he thought morosely. Now, possibly, drugged coffee. And there wasn't a thing he could do about it.

It was incredible that something like this should be happening to him, an officer of a national bank, a certified public accountant with a Yale law degree, an ordinarily efficient junior executive who'd left the bank that morning expecting to routinely serve an eviction notice on some hard-luck widow in the mountains. Nothing more complicated than that. Now, by some totally freakish turn of events, here he was, a virtual prisoner in this hillbilly backwater.

But at least, Greg told himself grimly, he knew who was responsible.

Five

JULIA PUT ON JIM'S OLD SHEEPSKIN COAT, slung the bucket of grain mash for Miss Piggy over her arm, and started for the barn. The wind was up; halfway there, the blowing snow made it so hard to see that she found the only way she was going to make it to the barn was to grab the old clothesline and follow it to the barn door.

So, Julia thought as she slid back the bar, stepped inside, and a blast of wind slammed the barn door behind her, at least one story about blizzards was true. Without a clothesline or a rope or something like that to hang onto, you could get lost virtually in your own backyard, wander away, and be found later, frozen to death.

Very cheerful, Julia, she told herself. Actually, she felt a bit better. The exercise, along with a goodly amount of freezing air gulped into the lungs, made the world look different.

It smelled different, too. The barn, built to stay warm with the animals' body heat, was also fragrant with ammonia and the overpowering sweet smell of stored hay. She stopped at General Lee's stall and put down the bucket of mash. The mule stuck his massive gray head over the top railing and nuzzled her hand, looking for sugar. She opened the sheepskin coat and took a plastic sandwich bag full of sugar lumps out of the inside pocket. When she shook them out into her gloved palm the mule pulled back his lips, exposing huge yellow teeth, and deftly scooped them up.

General Lee was something of a pet, if you could call anything with his cantankerous disposition that. The mule hadn't done a day's work in fifteen years; Grandpa Stonecypher had kept the General long after he'd given up cultivating his annual patch of corn and beans. Grandpa just hadn't been able to bring himself to send General Lee to the mule market in Atlanta, which seldom traded or sold mules these days; the old farm animals were sold instead to canneries for dog food.

The mule lowered his head over the barrier of the railing and butted Julia's arm. It had taken Julia a long time to get used to the General after Jim died. The old mule had sometimes tried to bite her when she fed him, until she found the way to his heart with sugar lumps.

On the other hand, the General was not to be taken lightly. There were stories about the mule's violent dislike of strangers, including the family favorite of how he had once chased the county agricultural agent through a pasture, kicking and whinnying, his long teeth bared, until the county agent finally had to take a running dive at a barbed wire fence to get away from him.

Although being butted by that hard gray head for sugar sometimes got too rough for Julia's taste, she had learned it was General Lee's version of a love pat.

She reached through the rails to scratch him between the eyes. "You're out of luck, General, no more sugar, it's all gone." She hadn't thought yet about what she would do with General Lee when she had to leave. "But then it looks like we're *both* out of luck," she said more softly. "I hate to tell you this, but this may be your last Christmas here."

As quickly as she could, hampered by Jim's big coat and her gloves, Julia filled up the General's feeding bucket with oats and stuck it on the hanger. At the next stall, she put down Miss Piggy's dinner again to pull a bale of hay from the crib. She spread it for Daisy, the cow, who was not being milked as she awaited the birth of her calf.

Before Julia was through forking hay through the bars, hungry Miss Piggy, smelling her grain mash, was running back and forth next door, alternating imperious grunts with ear-piercing, operatic squeals.

"You're such a prima donna!" Julia yelled over the racket. Poor, placid Daisy, sandwiched in between the irascible General and Deenie's purebred pig, never had a chance. "Sorry, Daisy," she told the cow, "I'll bring you an apple tomorrow. I just hope I don't have to shovel my way through six feet of snow to get here."

Tomorrow is Christmas Eve, Julia told herself as she made her way to the next stall. *Tomorrow!*

She dumped the Purina grain mash into Miss Piggy's trough, then used the bottom of the empty bucket to scratch the shoat's sleek white rear. Miss Piggy, her front feet daintily placed in the trough with her food, attended to dinner.

If getting rid of Grandpa Stonecypher's pet, the General, was going to be a problem, Deenie's beloved Miss Piggy was a crisis of national proportions. The pig represented Deenie's long hours of really admirable work and care—even though Deenie made up stories about her pig as she did about everything else, Julia thought, sighing. As, for instance, Miss Piggy had been a princess, long ago, put under a magic spell by a witch who'd come to her royal christening; at the county fair next year, she was going to meet a pig who was under an enchantment, too, but was really a prince waiting for her. . . . Deenie's imagination was endless.

Still, Julia thought as she watched the pig bury her snout in the still-warm mash, her child had worked faithfully with Miss Piggy. The 4-H project got scrubbed with Palmolive dish detergent at least once a week if the weather was warm enough, and Miss Piggy got fed not only the best grain mash Raeburn Gap's feed store carried, but she had also developed a gourmet taste for bananas, jellybeans, and CheezWhiz served a dollop at a time on potato chips. Miss Piggy was so spoiled it was hard not to wonder if she was living up to her television namesake.

Julia sat down on a bale of hay while the animals ate. She would have to have someone, probably one of the Makim's Mountain people who still did a little farming, come in and help her dispose of the livestock. Daisy could go to the auction and be sold—as a springer expecting to freshen soon with a calf, the cow would easily bring in several hundred dollars. Royal Miss Piggy could go quietly if the county 4-H office would buy her back, or supply her with a new owner. But the General . . .

I'm not going to cry, Julia told herself. Whoever cried over a nasty, mean old mule? But it's just so unfair, to have to get rid of the poor animals; they haven't done anything. It's not their fault I've failed, and we have to leave Grandpa's place.

Miss Piggy was now standing on four feet in her trough, pursuing the last of her dinner. Julia bent and picked up the feed bucket to carry it to the standpipe and rinse it out.

"Look what a mess you are now," Julia complained. "You know, if you really are a princess, Miss Piggy, you'd put in a good word for us with your fairy godmother. We certainly could use some help."

She dumped out the rinse water and slung the bucket on her arm. "I mean *all* of us could use some help," she pointed out. "You may be a pig princess, but you're in this, too, you know."

Miss Piggy, busy, didn't lift her head from the trough. But to Julia's surprise Daisy stuck her nose up against the rails and mooed. And on the far side, General Lee gave an indeterminate rumble.

"Thank you," Julia told them, laughing. "I knew I could count on you."

On her way out, General Lee rested his gray head on the rail, still looking for sugar. Julia shook her head at him. Before she sent the General to Atlanta, she was going to try to find a place for a mule nobody had any use for, even if she had to pay someone board to keep him. It was too much, at the General's age, to have to end up as dog food.

Going back, the wind was behind her, pushing her along at a run. Julia reached the back porch gasping with the cold air she'd swallowed. She was bending to slip off her snow-covered boots, hurrying to get out of the cold, when she heard voices inside. The deeper one was the loan officer's.

She stopped, her boot dangling, straining to hear them. *What was he telling her children?* She knew she shouldn't have left them alone with this man! She tore off the boot and threw it across the back porch.

She charged for the back door, not exactly sure what she would do. But she was ready to protect her little girls if she had to silence the loan officer with her bare hands. Just as she grabbed the door handle she heard Deenie's high, carrying voice asking what his job was.

Dear lord.

Before she could yank the door open, he answered in a low, cautious voice that he, er, dealt with numbers.

Julia froze, her hand on the knob. Numbers? He hadn't said he evicted people. He hadn't said he was going to take their home away from them.

Yet.

She put her eye to the crack, holding the door to keep it from blowing all the way open. Through the slit she could see they were at the big pine kitchen table, Emily Rose having climbed into his lap. Julia could just make out her yellow curls over the crook of his arm. She wasn't all that surprised; it would take an army to keep Emily out of any man's lap, especially one she called Daddy.

Deenie leaned from the opposite side, her eyeglasses shining. "Can you multiply—uh, four-six-seven-eight?" Julia's oldest child had just been introduced to the joys of fourth-grade multiplication; this was a real challenge. "Times—uh, one-eight-nine-nine," Deenie squeaked. "Oh—ah, *seven*?"

Julia knew she was doing an unforgivable thing by eavesdropping, and she was freezing on the windswept back porch, but she had to find out just what this man was up to. He mumbled, so she had to squeeze her ear to the door to catch it. "Eight million, eight hundred and eighty-three thousand," the loan officer said. "And five hundred and twenty two."

Deenie slid halfway across the big table in her excitement. "Oh, wow," she cried, impressed.

Julia was impressed, too. She pushed open the

back door. It sounded like the right answer, even though she had to admit she couldn't do something like that without a calculator. "I fed your pig, Deenie," Julia said loudly.

Her daughter never looked up. "I know you'd like one of my books," she was saying. "I'll bring it to you and you can read it. It's all about Christmas stories. I like Christmas stories—I like to read about Santa Claus and elves and things like that, don't you?"

"Deenie!" Julia unbuttoned the big coat and hung it on the nail by the back door. "Help me put some of these cakes in the freezer. Then you can set the table for supper."

"Oh, Mamma," her daughter cried, finally noticing her. "Do you know he can do arithmetic into the *trillions*? Just ask him to do a number, and you'll see he—"

"Daddy, Daddy," Emily Rose chanted. She got to her knees in the loan officer's lap and threw her arms around his neck. "Dadaaaaddy!"

"Deenie, I'm speaking to you!" He seemed to have her children's complete attention, while she might as well be talking to herself. "I want that table cleaned off right now."

The loan officer hadn't even bothered to turn. She noticed he wore his blond hair a little long. Either that or he was long past due for a haircut. Julia started for the pantry and the freezer, to take out some food for their supper.

"I'm not your daddy," he was saying to Emily Rose. "My name is Greg."

She scooped up packages of ham and vegetables

to put in the microwave and came to the door in time to see the loan officer pull Emily's arms down from around his neck. "If you call me daddy again, you can sit in your own seat."

Emily Rose looked at him thoughtfully, eyes veiled with sooty, inch-long lashes. "Daddy," she murmured, experimentally.

The loan officer stood up so fast the quilt dropped away from his hips, revealing white jockey shorts and an expanse of long, muscular legs.

Julia started toward them. "I'll take her!"

But he had already deposited Emily Rose in her high chair. Surprised, she regarded him for a long moment. Then Emily Rose opened her mouth. "Waaaaaah," she wailed, heartbroken.

Julia rushed to put herself in between them. "You don't have to talk to her like that! She isn't your child!"

"My point exactly." He looked at her over Emily Rose's head, his jaw set. "She's not my child. And I'm not her daddy."

"How could you do that!" she cried. "Can't you see you frightened her? Good heavens, you even enjoy being cruel to children, don't you?"

"Frightened her?" He scowled at her, blue eyes glittering. "I've never frightened a child in my life. Besides, this kid's got a will of iron. There are certain rules of behavior that can hardly be termed cruelty. Like not continuing to do something when an adult asks you to stop."

"You dropped her in her high chair!" Julia shouted. "I suppose you don't call that being cruel? Well, I want you to know, my children are not used to being mistreated!"

"Who's mistreated?" He had discovered the quilt down around his ankles and was furiously trying to pull it up to cover his underwear. "If anybody's being mistreated in this cuckoo environment, Mrs. Stonecypher, it's hardly your children. I'm suffering from a possibly dangerous concussion sustained in an automobile accident in front of your house, but I've had something less than what you'd call good physical care since you dragged me into this place."

"Dragged you into this place?" She stared at him, astounded. *"Dragged you?* Do you realize if I'd left you where you were, in your car, you'd be *frozen to death* by now?"

"Mommy," Deenie said, tugging at her arm. "May I speak to you, please?"

"I didn't ask to be taken here." He glared at her. "And, as a purely legal point, take note that I may even have been spirited inside this house against my better judgment."

Julia gasped. "Better judgment? Why, you were so anxious to get in here, you tried to flop yourself down on my living room sofa the very minute you came in! I practically had to pull you into Grandpa Stonecypher's bedroom to keep you from bleeding all over my floor! And then you—you—fell into Grandpa's bed and passed out without so much as a *thank you!*"

"I don't want to go into your possible motives in all this," he went on as though he hadn't heard her, "I haven't got all the facts sorted out. But I do want you to know that not only has my physical condition been virtually ignored by you, I've been pestered, constantly, by your children. One kid keeps climbing all over me, calling me her daddy. The other insists I'm some sort of Christmas fairy."

"Christmas *stranger*," Deenie said, looking up at him. "It's an old custom, Mamma knows it, to put a chair at the table at Christmas for the stranger who might come among us."

Behind them, there was a gusty sigh. A small voice said, softly: "Daaaaddy?"

The loan officer returned Julia's glare with a chilly smile. "I rest my case."

Deenie tugged again at her mother's arm. "Mommy, while you were out the 'frigerator went *rrrrrr, rrrrr*. So I put one of the lamps on the table. But you'll have to check it for me."

"I never heard anybody say such a downright rude and nasty thing," Julia sputtered. "Especially when someone has taken you into her house and—and—probably saved your life. Especially when you consider, Mr. Harding, what you're trying to do to *us*!"

He drew himself up, scowling. "Trying to do to *you*? That's a laugh! Mrs. Stonecypher, I'd like to remind you that you've confiscated my clothes. In spite of my repeated requests for my personal property, you have yet to produce it. Do you notice I don't have any pants, or any shoes?" he demanded ominously. "That's what they do to prisoners, isn't it? Also, you tell me the telephone isn't working, and that it's impossible to get back to town because the bridge has been closed. Neither of these statements has been tested yet by me. But then I'm waiting for you to say something about my missing wallet."

Julia's mouth fell open. She didn't know how she was going to answer that.

Deenie put her arms around Julia's waist and rested her head against her stomach. "There it is again," she said, resigned. "The 'frigerator noise. While you were out in the barn, the lights went real dim, then they came back on. I don't think anybody noticed but me."

Somewhere an electric motor gave a loud *clunk* and then stopped. Startled, the loan officer looked down at Deenie and then at her mother. "What's that? Do you know what she's talking about?"

Seconds later, a motor in the utility room gave a small, dying wheeze. Without warning, they were plunged into darkness.

There was a long moment's silence.

"That," Julia said, "is what my daughter was talking about. We must have been having power trouble while I was at the barn. Now I guess the storm's just taken it out completely."

"My God," they heard the loan officer say.

"Daddy," a small, somewhat distant voice whispered in the pitch dark. "Daddy? *Daaaddy?*"

Six

"AND THIS PICTURE," DEENIE SAID. THE kerosene lamp spilled a mellow, golden light on the pages of the old book with its nineteenth-century steel engravings. "This picture is about the hawthorne bush at Glas—Glast-on-bury," she read solemnly. "It blooms every Christmas because Joseph of—Ara—Ara—"

"Aramithea," the loan officer said without looking up. He moved the kerosene lamp out of the reach of Emily Rose, who had been eyeing it thoughtfully. "Allegedly Joseph of Aramithea arrived in England, went to Glastonbury, and stuck his staff into the ground in the middle of winter, and the hawthorne staff began to bloom."

Deenie looked up, frowning. "You said you couldn't read my book of Christmas legends because your glasses are broken," she accused. "That's why I'm reading the stories to *you*."

"I just happen to know this one." He sat, elbows propped on the table, looking over his clasped hands at Emily Rose. She lifted her azure eyes to him, opened her mouth to say something, then thought better of it and started sucking her thumb. "Doesn't it say something in the book," the loan officer continued, "about the hawthorne bush still being there?"

Julia called, "Emily Rose, take your thumb out of your mouth." From her seat at the end of the kitchen table, she picked two foil-wrapped pound cakes from the stack in front of her and dropped them into the cardboard box at her feet. The freezer was full of cake; now she was going to try storing the rest in boxes on the back porch, which, thanks to the weather, was an excellent deep freeze. Maybe day after tomorrow, she thought, I'll get a chance to deliver them.

Julia looked down the table at the loan officer. "She hasn't sucked her thumb for months," she said. "Not until you frightened her."

He was examining another illustration from the book Deenie held up. "I didn't frighten her. I told her to stop calling me daddy."

He wasn't, Greg told himself, going to argue. There was enough going on at that moment that would be, in any other place, a major crisis. No power, no heat, no electricity to cook with or to run the pump in the well, which meant no running water. Under the circumstances, you would have to regard the kid's thumb sucking as highly irrelevant. "Go on with the story," he told the older girl. "What else is there in your book besides the Glastonbury hawthorne?"

She pointed to the black-and-white drawing of several medieval figures. "There's the maidens looking into a bowl of frozen water. That's done on Christmas Eve, so the water freezes into the face of the man you're going to marry." She put the book down on the table to turn the page. The leatherbound volume was almost too big for her to maneuver. "The next picture's the chair left for the Christmas stranger. See the dining room with all the chairs around the table and everybody having Christmas dinner?" She bent nearsightedly to the print. " 'A custom in the American South which is generally believed to be of British or—origen. In the spirit of the season, an empty chair is left at the Christmas table for the unexpected guest. The practice has been traced to the an-cient Jewish practice of the *El—Elijah chair* at the Pass-o-ver and other feasts.' "

Greg leaned back in his chair and picked up his coffee mug, looking under lowered eyelids at the woman at the end of the table as she continued to pack cakes. He studied her bent head, with the dark hair piled carelessly that made her neck look even longer and emphasized her nicely carved chin.

She was a good-looking woman, he couldn't help thinking, without having to work at it. That is, she wore no heavy makeup, push-up bra, the predictable stuff. As far as fashion went, the old cardigan and jeans belonged to someone who slept on urban street gratings. But there was also an interesting sort of self-sufficiency about her that you still found in most of these mountain people. Even these days. They still didn't seem to give a damn what people thought of them.

He watched her give the youngest child a wad of red ribbon and patiently show her how to knot it. He had to hand it to the Widow Stonecypher: whatever quasi-illegal schemes she was into, she coped. In the same situation, his friends' wives would have had massive nervous breakdowns. Build a fire? Cook in the fireplace? Haul water from a well? He could picture them hysterical, rushing around, complaining loudly. He'd sat through a lot of dinner parties where the talk was of the trauma wives suffered when the Mercedes broke down and one of the kids missed ballet class.

"This," the little girl across the table said, holding up the book, "is about the Christmas stranger. It's a poem. You know it's a poem," she explained earnestly, "because the lines go in and out instead of across the page. See?"

"Perfectly," Greg told her.

In spite of everything, dinner had been amazingly good: ham slices with pan-fried potatoes, prepared in some sort of iron skillet with legs on it that was placed right in the embers, a vegetable casserole—or stew, actually, since it was cooked in a pot, in a very good cream sauce. Coffee made on the hearth, apple pie from the freezer thawed in a black pot with a lid on it. He'd watched the whole procedure, knowing it was more than good for a dinner she'd apparently intended to pop into the microwave oven before the electricity went out.

On the whole, he thought, watching her move another stack of cakes closer to wrap them in foil, you couldn't ask to be more comfortable caught here in the mountains in a blizzard. His friends wouldn't believe it, but it was true.

"I'm going to read it," the child across the table said. "Is it all right if I read it?"

"Um," Greg said. When she bent forward, the Widow Stonecypher's tailored shirt gaped open, revealing a silkily attractive view of her rounded breasts that left him totally distracted. He wondered what she did to keep that figure, that tiny waist. His friends' wives were always dieting.

Greg remembered the first hazy glimpses of her he'd had waking up in the bedroom. A gorgeous vision. Coming out from under, she'd seemed almost eerily lovely, yet at the same time warm and utterly fascinating. He had never reacted to a woman that way before, and he'd been surprised at how strongly it had grabbed him. Lying there with his head hurting so badly it nearly blinded him, he still had wanted to pull her right down in the bed with him and make love to her.

Until the moment, of course, he'd seen her lift his wallet.

"Here goes," the child said. She lifted the big book to prop it on the table, and read:

> *Candle, candle, burning bright,*
> *In our window late tonight,*
> *See the shining Christmas star,*

Calling shepherds from afar,
Lead some weary Traveler here,
That he may share our Christmas cheer.

"But Mommy won't let us have candles in the
windows, she says they're a fire hazard. Besides—" She looked up at him shyly, the golden
light from the kerosene lamp glinting on her eyeglasses. "We didn't have to have a candle in the
window when you came. You found us all right."

"Um," Greg said again. He'd been studying the
kitchen, turning in his chair to see all of it. He
knew James Stonecypher had been working on
the old family place when he died, but he hadn't
known the extent of the remodeling. The two
home-improvement loans, an unwise bit of lend-
ing his uncle had approved, were among the many
debts that had put this place in the bank's hands.
That and the lack of any insurance money due to
the nature of Stonecypher's accident. He couldn't
understand why a man with a wife and two kids
thought he had any business tooling around the
countryside on a racing motorcycle.

But the kitchen–family room was quite a nice
bit of work. Stonecypher had apparently done the
remodeling himself, and it had all the earmarks of
a professional job. The walls were stripped down
to original log construction in some places, freshly
plastered over in others, giving the room a very
authentic, rustic southern-mountains look that
you couldn't duplicate now with modern construction, Greg knew, for under a couple of hundred thousand. According to one of Stonecypher's

loan applications, the massive fieldstone blocks that formed the fireplaces had been freshly sand-blasted and the fireplaces themselves had been opened up after years of disuse, to be refitted with new flues.

This huge fireplace looked like one of those double systems in colonial houses that opened both in the kitchen and in the living room out of the same wall; it must have been the center of the original stone and log structure.

It was a lifesaver for them at the moment. He'd had some experience himself with power outages, and nonworking thermostats, that could turn even a modern house into an igloo. But with a roaring fire, and the double stone-log walls sur-rounding them, they might as well have been en-joying après-ski in some posh Aspen lodge. Or better yet, some restored mansion kitchen in Wil-liamsburg.

A glimmer of an idea flickered through his mind and Greg tried to pursue it and bring it back.

Meanwhile, the little girl had slid halfway across the table on her stomach holding her book. "This is the picture of the animals talking at midnight." She sent her mother a somewhat furtive look. "It says all the animals in barns come together at midnight on Christmas Eve," she whispered, "and they talk about how they've been treated all year, and if people have been good or bad to them. We have a mule and a cow in our barn. And I've got a pig from the Four-H, Miss Piggy, she's my special project this year. Don't you think it would be wonderful if we could hear what the animals have to say?"

"Sure." Greg was watching the sexy curve of Julia Stonecypher's rear as she hauled a box of cakes across the kitchen floor to the door.

Moments after the electricity had gone out she'd gotten all the kerosene lamps together. It seems the lamps were always kept filled and trimmed out here on the mountain, because if it wasn't ice and snowstorms in the winter, it was thunderstorms in the summer.

After lighting the lamps and getting the children to sit down, she'd brought in logs and lightwood before he could volunteer to help, set a fire, and got it going. It was obvious she'd been setting fireplace fires all her life.

The older child wriggled closer, clutching her book. "This Christmas Eve I want to go out to our barn to hear the animals talk," she told him urgently. "I just know they talk, but I've never met anybody who's heard them. Would you like to go with me?"

"Anytime," Greg said absently. He was thinking again of that idea he'd had about the whole Stonecypher business. It kept nagging him.

She'd managed the cranes and hooks and spiders and all the other complicated equipment of hearth cooking with a quick, efficient grace. She was going to have to do it again, in the morning, for breakfast, yet so far he'd heard no complaints.

Greg had never seen a meal prepared over leaping flames in a fireplace before. It looked—*was*—formidable. Of course, it had been done for centuries, but until now he hadn't been aware of the skill or the timing involved. It was a lost American art, a priceless American heritage.

He knew he was thinking in the sort of glossy language his father's ad agencies used for the bank's development campaigns. But something there rang true nevertheless. The condominium project slated for this very piece of property needed to be marketed right, if they were going to make anything of it this far up here in the mountains. The condominium-resort market wasn't what it had been in the eighties.

"Will you go with me?" the child in front of him was saying. "Mommy will let me go if you go, too."

"Sure," Greg said. He looked around the kitchen. "How about getting down off the table?"

Why did he keep thinking about Williamsburg? Stonecypher had left the old-fashioned handle pump by the sink, a nice touch, although the rest was modern, equipped even with what apparently was a garbage disposal. There was a pantry where, he gathered, the freezer and other appliances were stored. Yet for all of the modern touches, the room lost none of its authentic charm. *A lost American art. A priceless American heritage.*

Terrific, Greg Harding realized suddenly. *That was it!*

Julia came in from the back porch red with cold. The warmth of the kitchen was unbelievable. She remembered that she had wondered, at the time when Jim was renovating them, if the old fireplaces would really keep them completely warm in a storm like this. She wished he were here to see the results of his work.

"Mamma," Emily Rose announced, already climbing out of her high chair, "I get down."

"Yes, it's time to go to bed." Julia swung her daughter up and settled her on her hip. "Deenie?"

Her older child and the loan officer were bent over the old book of Christmas legends, their heads almost touching. He was wearing Jim's jeans, the blue shirt and some old bedroom slippers that were, surprisingly, a little too snug for his feet. *He does so little, and yet what he does,* she thought, biting her lip, *interferes with everything.*

"This is a very fine old volume of—whatever it is." He turned the pages. "Ah, here it is, *Christmas Legends In America,* published in eighteen seventy-six. With all these engravings, I would say it's worth some money. Your daughter tells me it belonged to one of the family, a Mr. Redlaw."

Julia pulled Emily Rose's thumb out of her mouth. "No one's interested in the money it's worth, Mr. Harding," she said, letting her distaste show. "It's an heirloom. It belonged to my husband's great-grandfather, who *read law.* Redlaw wasn't his name. That's just one of those things Deenie gets mixed up."

"Did he ever become a lawyer?"

Julia bent, still holding Emily Rose, to take the edge of the big book with her free hand and snap it shut. "That was the way one studied to be a lawyer in those days in the mountains. It cost too much to go away to the university, so if you wanted to be a lawyer, you apprenticed yourself as a clerk to some lawyer and 'read law.'

"Deenie, take your book and get ready to go to bed now," Julia told her. "Great-uncle Amos Stonecypher rode all over these mountains on horseback, practicing law. Even over Makim's Mountain to the valley on the far side. That's why the bridge was built; people used to go over the Gap. But then the Interstate was built and the mountain traffic died out, except for the summer visitors."

Julia felt the warmth rising to her face again. She didn't know why he looked at her like that. She supposed it was the wallet she'd taken. Well, when she put the girls to bed, she would have to give it back to him and apologize for taking it in the first place.

"There are lots of books in the attic." She wanted this arrogant banker to know that not all mountain people were ignorant and uneducated, as it was plain he thought they were. "More books than will fit in the bookcases downstairs. My husband used to go up there and read as a boy. He said it was better than any library."

With Emily Rose on her hip, Julia shepherded Deenie into the living room. The fire burning there shared the same flue and metal panels Jim had installed for radiant heat as the kitchen hearth. But the main room, being bigger, was not quite so warm.

"We're going to have to make some different sleeping arrangements," Julia said, "since the furnace won't be working with the power off. I've shut off the top part of the house and the bedrooms up there to save heat. The girls and I will sleep downstairs in Grandpa Stonecypher's bedroom. The bed is big enough to hold all three of us, and there's a fireplace in there, too. You're going to sleep out here. I thought you could help me pull the sofa over in front of the fire."

He ran his hand through his hair, forgetting, and winced. "You don't have a battery-powered radio, do you?" When she shook her head, he frowned. "I'd really like to know how long we're going to be in this mess." Abruptly, he turned from her and walked to the living room window. "There's a radio in my car. I wonder if I could get out to the road and back without having you send out the Mounties for me?"

The idea sent a chill of fear through Julia. As long as he didn't do anything reckless, she could survive having the loan officer with them overnight. But she didn't want to have to account for any corpses when the storm was over.

"Why don't you wait until morning?" She shifted Emily Rose's damp weight against her; the baby had gone to sleep in her arms. "Maybe we can rig something up then, like a rope you can use to get out to the car and back."

"Good idea." He sounded gloomy. "Well, we can't stay shut up here forever. Tomorrow's got to be the turning point." He cocked his head, looking at Emily Rose sleeping with her thumb in her mouth. "After you put them to bed, come back and we'll fix up the couch for the night. And—oh, yes," he called, as Julia started for the bedroom, "bring a flashlight, will you?"

Julia turned, Emily Rose on her shoulder and a sleepy-eyed Deenie by the hand. "Flashlight? What for?"

He leaned one arm on the mantelpiece and gave her an enigmatic look. "I'll show you when you get here."

Seven

JULIA DRESSED HER LITTLE GIRLS FOR BED in their thickest flannel "granny" nightgowns, reminding them why they were sleeping downstairs. "You're down here to keep warm," she said, "and sleep, not lark around, hear?"

It didn't do much good. The excitement of taking a sponge bath in the chilly bathroom, drying off in front of a roaring fire in Grandpa Stonecypher's bedroom, the prospect of no television and no lights except for the muted glow of the kerosene lamps made for a giggly, unsettling experience, not to mention the presence of the loan officer. Julia had vetoed a request by both girls to have him come in and kiss them good night.

"Sleep with us, Mommy," Emily Rose demanded. "Sleep with us now!"

Julia pulled the quilts up to their chins. "I will in a little while. I still have things to do." As a precaution, she tucked in Emily Rose's side of the bed all the way to the foot; her youngest still slept in her crib, as she wasn't quite old enough yet for Deenie's junior bed.

Well, that takes care of that, Julia thought, straightening up and looking around the bedroom. *So far so good.* The girls had been fed, bathed, and put to bed—in a few minutes she'd join them—now all they had to do was stay warm during the night. It must have been hard to get a good night's sleep in the old days, with someone having to get up and down to tend to the fire. She could see, she thought ruefully, that she was going to have the opportunity to find out about it firsthand.

"Close your eyes, you two, and settle down." She reached for Deenie's *Christmas Legends* book. "Deenie, you know you're not supposed to take things to bed with you."

Her oldest clung to her book stubbornly. "He *liked* them, Mommy," she said. "All the Christmas legends. He let me read them to him. He said he was going with me to hear the animals talk on Christmas Eve."

Julia didn't have to ask who *he* was. "Well, we'll see about that," she told her. "He may be gone by tomorrow night."

When she reached for the book, Deenie held onto it. Her face showed a withdrawn, distant expression that meant trouble.

The kind of trouble we haven't had for some time, Julia sighed. She sat down on the edge of the bed, her hand still resting on the book. Her daughter's face, bare of her eyeglasses, looked sweetly vulnerable.

"The animals *do* talk on Christmas Eve," Deenie insisted. "Things like that happen, just like we got our Christmas stranger, Mommy. We weren't expecting anybody at all and then—bang! —there the Christmas stranger was in his car in the ditch, and you had to help carry him into the house because his head was hurt, and look after him. It was just like it said in the book, about 'weary Traveler sharing our Christmas cheer.' "

"Deenie—"

Her little face was set. "Things do come true if you believe in them enough, I *know* they do, Mommy. You'll see, our Christmas stranger is going to go out to the barn with me on Christmas Eve, and we're going to hear the animals talk. You and Emily Rose can come, too!"

Emily Rose had snuggled close to her sister in the big bed. "Animals talk, Deenie." She patted her sister's face comfortingly. "It's Christmas."

Julia took Emily Rose's hand and stuck it under the covers again. "Deenie," she said carefully, "just because you want something very much doesn't mean you can make it real. I talked to you about this before, remember?" *When Daddy died,* she added silently.

Deenie wasn't listening.

"They're not just in books. Lots of people believed, long ago. That's why they became stories. There were lots and lots of Christmas strangers in the old days, and people took them into their houses *all the time*. Besides, how did people know the animals talked on Christmas Eve unless they heard them, lots and lots of times? Then they got to write it down." Her voice had risen. "That's how they got Christmas legends. Things do come true, Mommy, they *do*!"

That same pitch of voice, if not the same words. *My daddy's in the hospital, he's coming home someday soon.*

Emily Rose put both chubby arms around her sister's neck and hugged her. "Don't be thaad, Deenie," she lisped.

Julia watched her girls with despair. *If you believed in anything long enough, you could make it come true.* By now, they should know how wrong that was.

She said, "I think I'd better talk to our Christmas stranger about this." It was certainly something she wanted to discuss with him, she thought grimly. "His name is Greg—you heard him tell Emily Rose that his name was Greg, and I think we'd all better start calling him that. We'll see about all this visiting animals on Christmas Eve. I don't really know what he agreed to. Deenie, as I said before, he may not be here. They may open the bridge tomorrow, and then he'll go home."

Her daughter slid back down under the covers, unconvinced. "He'll want to do it, I know," she whispered. "If anybody can hear the animals talk, *he* can."

Julia stood up. It was all his fault, promising a child talking animals. A legend out of a book only made for certain disappointment. It was down-right cruel.

"Deenie, I want you to promise me you're not going to make a fuss about this," she said. "I know you think a lot of your Christmas stories, but enough is *enough*! Do you hear me?"

Her child looked over her shoulder into the distance. "Yes," she murmured. "Mommy, don't let the fire go out. Don't let it go out while we're asleep."

A new worry. "Good heavens, Deenie, I'm not going to let it go out."

Julia crossed to the fireplace and bent and lifted a log from the woodpile and rolled it to the back of the blaze.

"Now everything is just fine. So we're not going to worry." The sound of her voice was usually enough to chase away the regular bedtime demons. "We're safe in this big old house—the storm can't get to us. We're safe as a bug in a rug," she said, trying to make a small game of it, as she hung up the poker on its rack.

"Bug in a rug," Emily Rose's voice repeated from the big bed.

"And warm as toast," Julia said, getting her red velveteen robe out of the closet along with her slippers. *What else was there?* "And thick as fleas."

Not as good, but Emily Rose liked it. "Fleas!" she crowed.

"Happy as pigs in a puddle," Julia said, bending to pull off her socks and put on the slippers. "Or

. . . uh . . ." Good heavens, she had to come up with something. "A fox in a henhouse!"

Emily Rose dissolved in giggles.

"Happy as ants at a picnic," Julia said, searching for the nightgown she'd brought down from upstairs and laid on the bed. "And—what else?"

There was a silence.

Deenie's voice said, finally, "Larks. Happy as *larks!*"

"Larks!" Emily Rose said, promptly climbing into the middle of the bed to bounce up and down.

Julia smiled. She went to the bed to stop Emily Rose's bouncing and cover her up again. "Yes, we're happy as larks. That's my good girls." She bent to kiss them one last time, then she turned down the wick in the kerosene lamp and the room grew dim.

"Christmas comin'," Emily Rose breathed, snuggling up tightly to her sister. Deenie lay still on her back, her eyes wide and sleepless.

Julia straightened the bedcovers, quickly turned her older daughter on her side, rubbing between her narrow shoulder blades until she felt her small body relax, then pulled the covers up again.

"Yes," Julia murmured, "Christmas is coming."

In the bathroom, the tension that had lingered all day suddenly gripped her shoulders and neck so that the muscles knotted painfully. So much had happened, starting with that morning, when she'd rushed out into the driveway to intercept the loan officer, through his automobile wreck, down to the moment, Julia supposed, when the power had failed and they had found themselves back in the days when life was lived without "modern conveniences."

She shook her head at her image in the bathroom mirror. There was still no way to describe it, except that they were still in one piece, all of them, and still *there*.

Not everything was fine, of course. Deenie was worried that the fire would go out in their room and let in the cold and the dark. We're still not ready, Julia thought, to leave Grandpa Stonecypher's house. Just as we weren't ready to lose Jim.

Quickly, in the dim glow from the lantern, she stripped down to her underwear and bathed in some of the icy well water she'd carried into the bathroom earlier. She unpinned her hair and, shivering a little from her sponge bath, brushed it until, full of electricity, it floated from her face and shoulders in a dark cloud. Then she shrugged into her nightgown and robe.

She peered at her face in the mirror, seeing that her skin was pink and glowing from the hasty, cold-water scrubbing. She fastened the frogs of the red gown up to her chin, then spent a few minutes more brushing her teeth, rinsing with a cupful of the rationed water.

She'd been thinking for several hours that there ought to be something she could do for her children—some way, now that she had the loan officer there in her house, to fight what was happening to them. Looking over the day now past, Julia could see she'd made a mistake rushing around, accepting each thing as it happened.

She didn't know what on earth had caused her to think that Gregory Harding had amnesia after his wreck and wasn't going to remember who he was. It was as foolish as thinking he'd stay that way, and that she'd better take his wallet away from him to keep him from finding the truth!

In spite of herself, she sighed. When you came down to it, he was right. She *hadn't* paid her rent. Put that together with the stolen wallet and you could see why he had a terrible opinion of her. No wonder he'd acted so rude and suspicious.

What was almost as bad was that she'd been so panicked she hadn't stopped to think. If she had, she could have taken the bull by the horns and asked the loan officer if there wasn't some way the bank could give her time to catch up on her debts. Instead, she'd practically stampeded when he'd given her the eviction notice.

There weren't many alternatives, she realized. She didn't know if you could get a lawyer and go to court to fight an eviction. She supposed you could; it seemed like you could get a lawyer for just about everything these days. But the bank *had* been lenient to let her stay on after Jim died, in spite of all the money still owing on Grandpa Stonecypher's property. She supposed a judge would take that into account.

Anyway, she didn't have enough money for a lawyer. Even one in Raeburn Gap, where most of the lawyers wouldn't charge Jim Stonecypher's widow much, would be unaffordable. No, there was only one left thing to do, Julia told herself. She just didn't know whether she could bring herself to do it.

You'll do it for your children, Julia Stonecypher, her inner voice spoke up, *you know you will. You don't need a lawyer, and you don't need to go to court. What you need to do is go out there and talk to Mr. Gregory Harding himself about it.*

She stood staring at her lantern-lit reflection in the mirror. She needed to ask him to take back the eviction notice and give her a few months more, at least until the children got better accustomed to leaving everything here. At least until she could find a job somewhere.

It wasn't that much to ask. After all, she'd pulled him out of his car when it could have caught fire and exploded. Then she'd taken him into her own home, put him to bed, given him clothes to wear, fed him a dinner he practically devoured, then supplied him with a warm, comfortable place to sleep.

You go out there, that inner voice reminded her, *and ask him to take back the eviction notice and give you a little more time.*

Not forever, Julia told herself. She didn't want to seem unreasonable. But for a few months, four months, even six months—that would be good enough. By that time she was sure she would have a job.

Julia smoothed the red velveteen robe over her breasts and down to her waist with both hands and took a deep breath. She looked all right, she thought a little nervously. Her face was flushed, and perhaps she should put her hair back up, as it looked pretty wild from the brushing. But she really didn't want to take all that much time.

"I'll do it," she said out loud.

Greg was on his knees poking experimentally at the fire when she came in, her arms piled high with blankets and sheets for his bed. He took a look, then looked again. At the second look, he got to his feet.

Pure magic, was all he could think.

Gone was the old sweater with the holes in it and the shirt and patched jeans, the dark hair wrapped severely around her head. Instead of a softly pretty woman here stood a tantalizing beauty in a red robe that turned her slim body into a bright, sensuous flame. The mist of her hair floated around her shoulders and the slightly flushed, perfect oval of her face. Dark brows arched over shadowed, sexy, dark eyes.

Greg Harding knew, when he could get his breath, that at any other time and in any other place, he would have wooed the beautiful Widow Stonecypher with candlelight and fine restaurants and symphony concerts, paraded her before his drooling bachelor buddies, then whisked her off for extended, passionate weekend skiing at Vail or Aspen. On second thought, he might have isolated himself with her at some luxurious hotel on a secluded beach in the Bahamas.

Instead, here he was, stranded in a snowstorm after having served her with a paper to evict her from her home. And she had lifted his wallet, appropriately enough, and taken his clothes.

It couldn't be any worse.

"Ah," he heard himself say, as he reached for the blankets and sheets, "let me do that."

She was looking uneasy. "Are you sure you can make up the sofa all right? It's best if you double the sheets and tuck them under the cushions in back. . . ."

"I can manage." He'd been watching her lusciously curving mouth. "I've slept on a lot of couches. That is, as a kid," he added awkwardly. "I don't make a habit of sleeping on couches. I'll be perfectly comfortable here." As she reached to take the bedclothes back he said, "No, really, don't do that. I can make up my own bed."

Confound it, he could hardly talk. She was having an amazing effect on him. *That's what the red robe is for,* he told himself cynically. *Remember the old line: Just relax while I slip into something comfortable?*

Well, no matter what she was setting him up for, he had his own agenda. There were things he wanted from the Widow Stonecypher. He planned to get them, too.

"You said you wanted a flashlight?" she was saying.

The flashlight. He'd almost forgotten.

"Mrs. Stonecypher," Greg said, dumping the bed linens on the couch. "May I call you Julia? Thanks," he said without waiting for her answer. The rest of the evening was going to be dedicated to the ideas he'd been formulating ever since dinner. This also happened to be the only time he would find to pick her brains. "I need you to help me with something very important. But first go get the flashlight, and we'll get that out of the way."

Before Julia reached for the flashlight, which hung on its hook by the back door, she stopped and pressed her hands to her face. She couldn't exactly put her finger on what was wrong with her. The minute she'd come downstairs and looked at the loan officer—Gregory Harding, she corrected herself—it was as though she'd stepped into some strange, invisible whirlwind. And you'd have to have been blind to miss the look on his face.

It was the robe, she thought uneasily. It shouldn't have made all that much difference; it practically covered her from chin to toe. She had a flannel nightgown on under it, too.

Still, the way his eyes had gone over her . . .

Julia turned the flashlight on to test its batteries. She'd been acutely aware of him standing there in Jim's blue plaid shirt and jeans, broad-shouldered, narrow-hipped, virile-looking. Particularly appealing with his streaked blond hair.

She stuck the flashlight in her pocket, beside Gregory Harding's wallet. Just because this man was stranded at her house didn't mean there had to be anything between them. She was a widow with two little girls. Just because she was wearing a robe, which might be misinterpreted, didn't mean anything was going to happen.

I'll just go in and give him his wallet back, Julia told herself. I'll stand at a distance. Then I'll do my best to beg him to take back the eviction notice.

No, first, she decided, I'll ask him what he intends to do with a flashlight. If he thinks he's going outside to his car or something foolish like that, he's got another guess coming.

Eight

"SIMPLE," GREGORY HARDING SAID. "I want you to take the flashlight and look into my eyes." He indicated a place on the sofa beside him with a pat of his hand. "In lieu of the emergency medical care I didn't get, I'm going to have to ask you to do this. Don't look so skeptical. I can assure you, this is really important."

"Oh," Julia said.

She'd hardly been looking skeptical; she was merely thinking this wasn't the way to begin a conversation about the loan officer's wallet. Which she fully intended to give back to him with an explanation about how she happened to take it.

Gathering the velveteen skirts of the robe around her, she sat down tentatively on the edge of the sofa cushions.

"I got quite a crack on my skull when the car hit that ditch," he was saying, "so it's important to find out whether or not my pupils are dilated. If they are, then I definitely have a concussion. That means I should be watched closely for about twenty-four hours and not be allowed to doze. Concussions are nothing to mess around with. It's too easy for the injured party to slide into unconsciousness and develop a clot on the brain or something equally severe. In my case, stranded out here on your mountain, that means I could possibly die."

When he got wound up, Julia thought, staring at him, he had a tendency to go on and on. She'd noticed the same thing that morning with his talk about banks and their regulations.

"Well, I really didn't know that," she said. "I mean about looking in your eyes, when I put you in Grandpa Stonecypher's bedroom. I'm sorry I let you stay unconscious so long."

"So am I." He moved closer on the sofa cushions. "But you can help me now. Here, take the flashlight. Take your thumb—" Before Julia could pull away he had grabbed her hand and pried open her fingers. His grip was surprisingly strong. "Take your index finger and spread them like this above and below my eye socket. Now, hold my eye open while you bring the flashlight up to it."

He had placed her finger above his eye and her thumb below so that his eyelids were held open with most of the eyeball exposed. Julia looked into it helplessly. She had never in her wildest daydreaming imagined she would be caught in such an intimate position with the Dalton bank's loan officer. But here they were, practically thigh to thigh on the living room sofa. He was much too close, but he didn't even seem to notice it, so intent was he on what he was doing. When he spoke his mouth was so near hers it actually whispered a breath against her lips.

Julia yanked her hand away.

"I don't really think I should be doing this," she said. "Why don't I stand up, and you can—"

He looked annoyed. "Look, I know what I'm doing. Besides, this is the least you can do, isn't it? Seeing as how I wouldn't be out here on Makim's Mountain in the first place, wrecking the bank's car on the ruts of that confounded dirt road outside, if it hadn't been for your delinquent rent."

"Yes, the r-rent," she stammered nervously. "That's something I'd like to talk to you about."

"Look—can we do this one thing first?" He seized the hand with the flashlight and dragged it back. "Do you know what a dilated pupil looks like?"

"Yes—no!" His fingers were right over the spot where her pulse was racing. "I guess they're— um, they're bigger, wider," she said desperately, "aren't they?"

"Exactly." He looked at her with some irony. "Listen, *I'll* hold my eye open, if that will make you feel better." He demonstrated. "Now all you have to do is hold up the flashlight and tell me what you see."

Julia looked uncertain. "Which eye?"

He made an exasperated noise. "The one I'm holding open, naturally."

"Oh. Yes, of course."

Julia lifted the flashlight and studied the depths of one round, black pupil. She was afraid to mention it to him because she didn't want to appear any more stupid than he apparently already thought she was, but how could she tell whether it was dilated or not, when she had nothing to compare it with? Did this one look, she asked herself, *enlarged*?

At the same time, she couldn't help noticing he was leaning into her at such an angle that he'd placed a hand on her thigh to brace himself. The touch through her robe was disturbing. She seemed to be touching *him*, too. Somehow she was sitting so that her breasts brushed the front of his chest through the plaid shirt. The tips of her nipples had tightened into hard pebbles, a reaction that was bothersome if not downright mortifying.

Very carefully, she moved back. Immediately, he tightened his grip on her wrist. "You'll have to sit still," he told her, "and not bounce around if you're going to see anything. Well, how about it?"

Staring at him like that, she was aware that her heart was beating wildly. She knew he could feel it with his fingers on her wrist, right over her racing pulse. He lowered her hand with the flashlight and sat looking at her with a curious expression.

They were leaning toward each other, his hand still on her thigh. They couldn't seem to look away. The moment stretched on.

"Damn," he said under his breath. His eyes, like blue fire, looked down at her mouth.

Something, Julia knew with a shudder, was going to happen if she didn't stop it. "Ah—you—your eyes—*eye*—is definitely dilated." Her words burst out in a rush. "Well, a *little*, I'd say. Compared with the other one. I mean, both of them."

He still stared at her.

She couldn't tear her eyes away, either. "You might have a slight concussion," she breathed.

"Slight concussion?"

"Yes—oh, yes!" Julia nodded rapidly. "Your eye was—the pupil was definitely larger than . . . before. Well, I mean, you can look at it now and see that it is."

He gave himself a slight shake. "Concussion," he repeated. "Yes, my eyes. Did the pupils shrink and get smaller when you flashed the light in them?"

Well, that much she *had* seen. His whole eye had flinched. "Oh, yes!"

"Then I guess I'll have to take the usual precautions." His gaze drifted over her, abstracted. "I need your cooperation. You'll have to stay up with me and see that I keep awake."

Julia's mouth fell open. "Why do that?"

"Why?" He frowned. "Look, I've just told you why—in case there are complications. It's not too good for my general condition to lie around here in a stupor."

"But you *haven't* been lying around in a stupor! Good heavens, you've been alert and awake, you ate dinner, and listened to Deenie read her Christmas stories—"

"You can spare me a few hours, can't you? After all, it's not such a big thing, talking to me and checking my eyes every so often to see if I'm all right."

Julia gulped and looked away. When he put it like that it was hard to refuse. Of course she didn't want him to slip into unconsciousness and die right there on her living room sofa.

On the other hand, she couldn't sit up all night! The long, hectic day, the worry and fatigue, the blizzard—and now the heat from the blazing fire—was making her so sleepy it took all the manners she could muster not to yawn in his face.

"Just sit here and talk to me," Gregory Harding told her. He leaned back among the sofa cushions and crossed his arms over his chest. "Don't let me go to sleep. That's not too complicated, is it?"

Julia bit her lip. Perhaps a few hours together in front of the fire would work out after all. She would give him back his wallet, overlook all his obnoxious games, like interfering with her children and pretending to lose his memory, and then she would have a chance to talk to him.

She saw that he had pulled one of the blankets over the sheets he'd spread at his end of the sofa. "Might as well get comfortable," he said, patting them. "I'll put some logs on the fire."

He got up and went to the hearth, jabbing the burning wood with the poker.

"You wouldn't happen to have any tea, would you?" he asked over his shoulder. "I'd like a hot cup of tea—sugar, no milk, thanks. You can bring in the stuff and make it right here on the hearth, can't you?"

Julia stood looking at him. A hot cup of tea—

sugar, no milk, thanks. Then she could sit up with Mr. Gregory Harding, the Dalton bank's loan officer, on the big living room sofa in front of the fire while she talked to him to keep him awake.

The trouble was she hadn't forgotten that strange chemistry of a few minutes ago. That odd, trancelike spell that had fallen upon them so inexplicably. It had seemed to hold them, staring into each other's eyes, as the minutes ticked on. Another second, she was certain, and he would have kissed her.

Another second, Julia told herself, irked, and she would have wanted him to. That was probably the worst thing that could happen to her right now. She hated to think what it would be like if Mr. Gregory Harding returned to his bank with a spicy story of being stranded in a blizzard with a hungry young widow who'd thrown herself into his arms.

What had happened was a warning to keep her distance down at her end of the sofa and not let those brilliant blue eyes, those strong hands, pull her any closer.

Something more important still needed her right now. If *she* could stay awake, she had a chance to talk him into letting her keep her house for a few more months.

A gust of wind blew down the chimney and sent a shower of sparks out onto the hearth and over Greg, who was kneeling there. He started, brushed at his clothes, then put the poker back on its hook and got to his feet.

The storm was really howling. At times, the wind hit the house with such force that it seemed on the verge of buckling the fortresslike old logs and two-foot-thick fieldstone, but he knew it was only a trick of air pressure.

He walked to the night-black window, rubbed a spot on the pane, and tried to see out. All that was visible out there was darkness and snow. Even a few feet back from the window glass one could feel the cold penetrating the room and the power of wind and snow blasting the mountainside.

The blizzard was holding them all in a strange, frozen time warp, he thought irritably, until it blew itself out and finally let them go. That would be, hopefully, sometime tomorrow. Until then they were isolated: two little girls, a woman, and a man.

Turning away from the window, he told himself everything seemed to be under control. But he was still restless. He looked at his watch. It was only eight o'clock. He missed seeing the television evening news. He missed getting the news about the storm on his car radio. Not to know what was going on was galling. He had to get out tomorrow, he told himself. One more day of this and he'd be climbing the walls.

He sat back down on the couch. Actually, one more day of this and he was in danger of doing something he might regret. For the continued sight of Julia Stonecypher, especially in that ruby red gown that clung so tightly to her slender body, was bound to bring on another moment like the one he'd just been through.

A near miss. Oddly enough, he'd never experienced anything like that before in his life. Whatever that momentary, pulse-pounding attraction had been, it was all he could do to keep from sweeping her up in his arms and carrying her to the nearest bed. The only way to avoid making a complete fool of himself, Greg thought testily, was to get back to business.

He stretched out his feet before the blazing fire. He'd had a good enough idea earlier, in the kitchen, about the projected future of the Stonecypher place. The condo project had always lacked a center, and it seemed he'd just found it.

Originally the development concept had a Swiss theme: each unit was to be a two-story chalet closely resembling the floor plan of the ever-popular town house, but these would be constructed of concrete block and oak-stained timber. Authentic down to the architect's sketch of attractive window boxes filled with brilliant alpine-type blooms.

The Swiss look, according to the Atlanta firm of architects the bank had hired, had been chosen because of the Makim Mountain setting. Mountain living was the motif. In fact, the projected clubhouse and inn was a copy of an actual villa outside St. Moritz.

Then, this evening, watching Julia Stonecypher, Greg had suddenly seen the idea in a whole different light. Why go all the way to Switzerland when the real thing was right here? This was the real America—not some borrowed European prototype with fancy jigsaw work and flower boxes.

He got up and paced back and forth in front of the fire. He ran his hand through his hair, and flinched. He had forgotten again. There was still a lump the size of a golf ball on his head.

When he thought of the bank's condominium project, what he remembered was not the few Swiss skiing trips to Davos and Klosters he'd taken, but the times as a kid he'd gone hunting in these mountains with his grandfather. Once, during his college days, he'd hiked over the Gap to the other side of the mountain to camp out on Bobcat Creek and had been run off in the middle of the night by a bunch of moonshiners. They'd found him sleeping practically on top of their still without even being aware of it. It was something to tell his grandchildren about. He'd been scared out of his wits.

Now, he was sure, the only thing to do was scrap the plans for the grandiose Alpinehaus Condominiums and Matterhorn Inn and start over again.

What the bank's development needed were authentic, American-designed luxury living units up here in the beautiful hills that reminded you of your roots. A cosy place to hole up in when a mountain snowstorm trapped you in winter. Or a summer thunderstorm lashed the earth. A place warm and earthy, like a beautiful woman with dark, mysterious eyes and dreamy lips.

Off the track again, Harding, he told himself. Stick to the subject, or you'll be low man on the totem pole in your family's bank, evicting widows and orphans for the rest of your life.

There had to be a better way, he thought, suddenly morose; this trip up the mountain had proved that. Serving eviction papers had to be the pits in anyone's life. Still, he couldn't see any way out for a while. Not if he had to pick up on his uncle's ill-fated loan policy, bail it out, and keep the condo investment from going under at the same time. There were some things, when you were vice-president of a family-owned bank, that you just didn't whine about.

Julia came in with a tray that held a copper kettle full of water, a tin tea cannister, a small jug of milk, and the sugar bowl. She saw the loan officer on the sofa with his long legs sprawled out in front of him, the too-tight bedroom slippers kicked off, staring thoughtfully at the roaring blaze.

She put the kettle on the crane and swung it over the fire. "We'll have some tea in about ten minutes," she said.

"How did you learn to do that?" He didn't look up. "All the things you did for dinner tonight, cooking in the fireplace. And right now, putting the kettle on that thing to make tea."

After a slight hesitation she sat down beside him. "Cooking over a hearth fire is simple. You just have to get used to different equipment. You hang the pots by their handles on cranes and then swing them over the fire. They go directly into the fire for quick cooking, to one side for slower heat. The skillets and spiders either have legs of their own so you can put them right on the coals, or you put trivets under them. I haven't done much spit roasting," she confessed. "I haven't got the time to sit and tend a spit, and I don't want the girls too near the hearth when there's an open fire. I don't let Deenie do it, and she wants to, so much."

He turned to face her.

"Although I imagine girls of Deenie's age," Julia continued, "turned the fireplace roasting spit quite a lot when this house was first built. My great-great-grandmother told my mother that she could remember having to do it when she was a girl—even working the dash to churn butter with the other hand."

"And your mother taught you." His blue eyes were very intent.

"Goodness no!" She had to laugh. "My mother was a schoolteacher. She never cooked in a fireplace in her life. I picked up pioneer homecrafts at Berry School, when I was a student there."

Julia was sure he would know the famous school founded by Martha Berry over half a century ago to educate mountain children. Most people did.

"When I was there we were always being asked to do demonstrations of mountain skills and handicrafts, mostly for fairs and exhibitions. I can weave, too; it's my hobby. I had a loom set up before Emily Rose was born, but I had . . ." Julia's voice faltered. "I had my husband take it down when she was a toddler."

"Was he at the Berry School?" He was watching her face. "Is that where you met him?"

She looked away. "No, Jim didn't go there. He went to Raeburn Gap High School and then to

Gainesville to study welding. He'd always wanted to open a business of his own and stay in the mountains."

The kettle began to whistle and she got up. "So many young people don't stay," Julia said. She put a handful of tea in the bottom of the china teapot, tilted the kettle, and poured boiling water into it. "It's been a big problem. Kids who graduate from high school here go away to the cities where they can earn a living. That just leaves too many old people up in the mountains for the young people to send money back to. In some of these counties, half the people are on welfare."

He took the cup of tea from her. "Why didn't your husband's welding shop work out?"

She stiffened. "My husband was a very smart, hardworking person, Mr. Harding. He was one of the finest people I've ever known. It was always his ambition to start a small business here and hire mountain people. He loved Raeburn Gap; he wanted to try to find a way to keep young people here. But times just got harder." Her voice dropped. "It seems like the mountains just get poorer. I told you I lost my job last week because the insurance agent I worked for just wasn't making ends meet."

Her hand went to the pocket in the robe where she'd put his wallet. *Now's the time,* she told herself. *While we're on the subject of money.*

"Aren't you going to have any tea?" he asked her.

"Yes, certainly." She fumbled with the teapot. "There's something I want to ask you—"

"I'm glad you brought this up, about unemployment up here and keeping people at work in the mountains." He held out his empty cup to her. "That was very good tea."

Julia put down her cup and saucer and reached for the teapot again. "I have to explain about this afternoon. Actually, I thought you really had lost your memory—"

"Oh, that." He took a sip of his tea and looked pleased. "I was groggy there for a moment when I came to, but things cleared up eventually. Look, what I want to ask you is, do you think you could teach these . . . skills of yours to someone else?"

Julia stared. "Skills?"

"Yes, everything you've done since the power went out. Cooking in the fireplace, getting the kerosene lamps ready. You said you weave. What kind of weaving do you do?"

Julia sat beside him with her cup of tea in her hand, not knowing what to say. Why was he asking her all this? Why did he admit, so easily, that he pretended he'd lost his memory? And what was his sudden interest in her weaving? If she explained it to him, she knew he wouldn't understand.

When she turned to him, the look on his face took her breath away. "Do you know how you look in firelight?" he said huskily. "You look like you've just stepped out of the last century."

"I—" Julia began.

Tell him, Julia's inner voice shouted at her, *that you need him to take his eviction notice back! Do it now before you start mooning into his eyes!*

114

But he spoke first. "That's the point—the last century. I see the bank's condo project here in a whole new light. The original design was Swiss, chalets and a sort of après-ski lodge motif for the projected inn, but after seeing you here in these surroundings—how old is this building, anyway? Early nineteenth century?"

Julia's mouth dropped open. He was talking about the bank's plan to build condominiums on Stonecypher land as though it was an accomplished fact. Probably, it was—the bank had foreclosed on Stonecypher property a year and a half ago. They owned it now.

Did that mean that talking to him about taking back her eviction notice was totally useless? She suddenly felt such an overwhelming wave of tiredness it was hard to hold her head up and not yawn. "Before the Cherokee's Trail of Tears," she said. "The original land deed was around eighteen ten."

"Really?" He looked at her with approval. "It's older than I thought, this place; it's practically a museum. I suppose the thick walls were in case of Indian attack."

Julia propped her head on her hand on the sofa's arm. "No, actually, Lucius Stonecypher's bride was three quarters Cherokee, and she—"

He jumped up and began pacing in front of the fire, stopping only to take a gulp of tea from his cup now and then. "From an essentially lackluster idea," he said, "that is, the Swiss chalet thing, to this authentic house is a real turnaround. I know I can sell my family on it!"!

Julia closed her eyes. The sound of his vibrant voice beat on her ears. *So you see,* she told herself wearily, *that's what it's come to.* He can't wait to get us out.

"Call it a lodge," he continued. The Appalachian *Lodge.* This living room right here can be expanded into a lobby, and there's enough fieldstone here on the mountain to build a wing to the lodge that would look just like the original structure. But here, this big common room, and the kitchen, and maybe that downstairs bedroom, which can be used as an office, is the heart of it. If you can teach a small staff, say the receptionist and the reservations clerk, how to do demonstrations of mountain cooking in the fireplace, that would be superb."

Julia opened one eye with effort. "Teach somebody how to cook in a fireplace? What on earth for?"

"Why, to do it the way they do it at Williamsburg," he said, turning to look at her. "Say, tell me, are you going to stay awake?"

She opened both eyes—just barely. *I'll stay awake if you'll talk to me about a roof over our heads for my children and myself.*

"I'd like to say something," Julia mumbled. "But you haven't given me a chance."

He threw himself down beside her and put his arms across the back of the sofa. "Wake up," he told her. "You have to stay awake and keep me from going to sleep, remember? Well, what do you think about it, the idea for the Appalachian Lodge? It's what we were talking about a little earlier, employment here in the mountains. The condos are going to provide jobs for construction workers. Then there's the condo and lodge staff itself, maintenance workers, groundskeepers, the golf course people. We'll put a priority in hiring local labor."

Sleep was fogging Julia's brain. But she was not so out of it that she didn't want to tell him what a lowdown, despicable person he was to be thinking about the bank's fancy condominium project when she and her family were going to be homeless. She just couldn't seem to get her words together. His voice droned on. Her head, even her body, was tilted, leaning against his arm, which had somehow come down from the back of the sofa.

"The idea of dressing up these people doesn't really grab me," he was saying, "but on the other hand, you can't beat it for authenticity. I seem to remember the backwoods people of Appalachia having a distinctive sort of clothing. . . ."

Through her exhaustion, it seemed a thousand ideas came and went with the determined sound of the loan officer's voice. Lodges and golf carts and maid service for the condos, even a landing pad for helicopters. The unemployment rate would drop. There would even be a broader tax base to provide schools.

She supposed she dozed off a little, because he was shaking her. "Are you supposed to be helping me keep awake?" his voice said, close to her ear. "You're really tired, aren't you?"

"Ummm," Julia murmured sleepily. As she

tried to say something more, a hand tucked a blanket around her and pulled her down against a warm, giving surface.

She supposed she slept, because in no time at all she was dreaming—of the big snowstorm that happened long ago, when she was a child, of Christmases, of moving into Grandpa Stonecypher's house. That was a strange dream. She walked from room to room, and they were bare of furniture, and she kept saying to herself, "So is my heart." Finally, she dreamt of Jim.

She was so glad to see him she wept. "Don't miss me so much, honey," he murmured, his mouth warm on the side of her cheek. "You can't go on grieving like that."

She turned into him with a sigh, aching with happiness just to feel his big, hard body against hers again. She wanted him to kiss her. When she reached for his mouth he seemed to laugh, tenderly.

She could feel his lips against hers. His hands held her waist, pressing her body to him.

Don't leave me, Julia cried. *Don't ever leave me again!*

I gotta, hon. Jim's voice was a little reluctant. *What's going to be is going to be. Besides, that's some other man's arms around you.* That same warm, husky laugh. *Not mine.*

Julia's eyes flew open.

"Mommy," a voice said from the doorway, "the fire in Grandpa's bedroom's going out."

Julia couldn't get awake fast enough. That was

Deenie, wanting something. But she was lying under a weight almost too heavy to move. A man's body, she realized, panicked.

The living room was slightly chilly. Gregory Harding had pulled the blanket over both of them. Snuggled together in front of the fire, they had somehow managed to slide down side by side until they were lying together on the sofa. He was asleep.

Her dream hadn't been wrong—she'd been sleeping in his arms! One of her legs was trapped intimately between his. His weight held her down against the sofa's back. His mouth had been pressed against hers. Her lips were burning.

"Mamma, what are you doing?" her daughter said, coming closer to peer at them, curious. "Is that our Christmas stranger with you?"

Gasping something incoherent, Julia threw off the blanket. She pushed his leg aside so that she could crawl out from under him.

"Shhhh," she managed thickly, "we don't want to wake him up."

As soon as she could get on her feet she grabbed Deenie's arm and hurried her in the direction of the bedroom.

"Was he kissing you?" Deenie's voice was excited. "Does he like you, Mamma?"

Julia couldn't get to the door fast enough. She was sure he was awake. He seemed well enough with or without his concussion. She was sure he was listening. Her face was burning.

"Because if he likes you," her daughter went on,

pulling away to look up into her face, "that's all right, Mommy. It really is."

"I'll discuss this with you later," Julia said hoarsely. "I promise I will. But for right now, Deenie, will you please not say anything more?"

Nine

THERE WAS NO PROBLEM, JULIA TOLD HERself as she fixed breakfast the next morning. She was not embarrassed or ill-at-ease over what had happened on the living-room sofa last night. In fact, it was no trouble at all to look squarely at Greg Harding when he came into the kitchen, and speak to him politely.

He was wearing the blue plaid shirt and jeans of the day before. When Julia handed him his cup of coffee, she saw he'd washed in cold water in the downstairs bathroom, because he had a ruddy, glowing look. He hadn't shaved because she hadn't thought to give him a razor, but he'd tried to spruce up by slicking down his hair. It still rose in stubborn, sun-streaked waves, especially on the sides and in the back.

Emily Rose promptly climbed onto his lap and leaned back against him comfortably, sucking her thumb. Deenie went for her Christmas legends book to read to him about Good King Wenceslas. So, Julia told herself as she slid scrambled eggs out of the skillet and onto a big platter in the center of the table, as far as the business of waking up in the loan officer's arms was concerned, it was unimportant. Nor was it necessary to try to remember the feel of his mouth—that kiss that never happened—on her lips.

She put a plate with eggs and cornbread in front of the older child. "Deenie, put down that book and eat your breakfast." Her eldest had taken to clinging to the volume of Christmas legends like it was some sort of literary security blanket. For the past few minutes, she'd noticed that when her daughter wasn't reading the account of how Good King Wenceslas had saved a poor beggar's life in the snowstorm, she was studying her as she moved from the fireplace to the table and back again, then Gregory Harding, who was sitting opposite. Julia couldn't help wondering if Deenie had seen more last night than she first thought.

But what was there to see? The only thing she'd been certain of herself when she opened her eyes was that she was stretched out on the sofa in Greg Harding's arms, her robe hiked up enough to feel his jeans-clad leg thrust between her bare legs. And his mouth . . . Well, his mouth had been pressed against her lips. She had felt the first fiery touch of his tongue, a sensual intrusion, and she remembered the kiss as ardent and powerful, just beginning to be demanding. Was it a real kiss, or was it just her imagination? The way her whole body had surrendered to it, it had to have been real.

"Could I trouble you for some more coffee?"

Julia jumped. She turned, the skillet still in her hand. Suddenly—now, when they couldn't avoid it, when they were all unprepared for it—their eyes met. After the first shock, something in his cobalt-blue gaze questioned her. She sucked in her breath.

"I'll get it!" Deenie cried eagerly. She put her book down and slipped from her chair. "I'll get the coffee pot."

"No, you don't." Julia still held the skillet in her hand, unable to break away from that blazing blue look. "Deenie, don't go near that fire!"

Locked in his gaze, she was trying not to remember all the strange dreams she'd had after she'd slipped into Grandpa Stonecypher's bed to lie between her sleeping children. Absurd, restless dreams. She'd been exhausted, but she'd dreamed she'd been working in a hotel, an inn, dressed in a fancy colonial costume, serving dinner for hundreds—a crowd big enough to fill a vast hall—and cooking it all in a fireplace big enough to stand in, assisted by an army of pages and cooks.

In her dream, George Washington—ridiculously enough, the general himself—had burst in. He went straight to her, his uniform still snow-sprinkled, to put his arms around her. Then it was not George Washington but a familiar, good looking man with fair hair and brilliant blue eyes who kissed her, and kissed her—it seemed as though those passionate kisses would never end. Trembling, undecided, she'd waited for Jim to come and say something to her as he had before, about sleeping in another man's arms. But nothing had happened.

"Why don't you let her get it?"

Julia came back with a start. "Get what?"

Emily Rose took her thumb out of her mouth and lifted her hand to pat his cheek. He caught her wrist and held it away. "The coffee pot. You don't seem to notice she wants to help you a lot more than you let her."

Aware that she had an ally, Deenie headed for the fire. "I know how to use the pot holder," she chattered excitedly. "I know how to swing the crane out—look!"

Before Julia could move to stop her, she'd unhooked the coffee pot. Frowning with importance, she carried it to the table. With both hands she lifted the heavy blue enamelware pot and filled his cup.

Julia had watched, ready at any moment to run and snatch the coffee pot away from her. Now she only said, "Put it back on the crane, please."

Greg was looking at her with the hint of a smile on his lips. "How are you feeling this morning?" he murmured as she sat down at the table.

Julia's lips clamped together thinly. He seemed to think it was funny, but her own daughter had disobeyed her, the first time in a long time. It would be different if he were a different sort of man, she fumed as she scraped the last of the eggs from the platter onto her plate. Like someone kind and genuinely interested. But he was a coldhearted, overbearing, money-grubbing, cynical monster; she'd found out last night that things she'd been raised to regard as important had no value for him. All he was concerned with was taking her home away from her and turning it into a touristy attraction for condominium guests!

"Wonderful breakfast." He wiped his mouth on his napkin and let Emily Rose slide out of his lap. "Cornbread, scrambled eggs, sausage—was that homemade sausage? It was delicious."

Julia didn't look up. She'd been wondering since she woke up that morning if she'd have one last chance to get into town and pick up the girls' gifts. One last chance to get rid of Greg Harding. But the wind was still howling around the corners of the house, and it was still snowing, even if some shift in the weather appeared to make the falling snow lighter and finer. She'd been able to get out to the barn early that morning to feed the animals without using the clothesline.

If the blizzard would only stop, Julia thought, closing her eyes. If only they could get to town! If only some power on high would give them a Christmas!

She opened her eyes to find that he'd been watching her. He abruptly pushed back his chair and stood up. I'm going out to my car. It's time to check things out."

"You're not going anyplace, are you?" Deenie jumped up from the table clutching her Christmas book. "Oh, please, you can't! It isn't Christmas yet!"

He reached out to ruffle her hair with his hand, but he was looking at Julia. "I'm going to listen to my car radio. First thing I want to check is the condition of the bridges and roads up here. I need some boots—I can't get out to my car in these bedroom slippers. I'll also need a heavy coat." He turned and looked at the sheepskin coat that hung by the back door. "Do you mind if I use that one?"

Julia followed him. "Do you think you should be doing this? What about your head? Isn't this bad for your concussion?"

"It's fine." He took down the sheepskin. "My head's all right."

"You should wear a hat," she insisted.

"It's still too sore. My scalp's full of lacerations, you should know that." He stuck his hand in the pockets of the coat. "I need the boots," he reminded her.

"Yes, the boots." She turned away. "I think there's a pair of Grandpa Stonecypher's boots in the downstairs closet. His feet were about as big as yours."

He was really going to try to get off the mountain. It was plain to her that he was going to look at his car to see if he could move it. She supposed he wanted out of there as badly as she wanted him gone.

"Don't do anything foolish." She trailed him into the big outer room, the girls following. "If you get into trouble out there. I don't know what we can do. I'm—I'm not certain I could come after you."

He gave her an enigmatic look. "My dear Mrs. Stonecypher, I certainly wouldn't want to put you to any more trouble than I already have."

There was no missing the sarcasm. But it was obvious he was anxious to at least try to leave. For some reason, the thought didn't make Julia as happy as she thought it would.

They watched him from the front living-room windows. The falling snow was icy, backed by a fierce wind. He leaned into it, the sheepskin collar turned up around his ears. At the mailbox the snow had drifted deep and they saw him suddenly drop into it like a swimmer stepping into a hole. Both girls screamed. Julia watched, the corners of her mouth turned down, wanting to laugh. It was comical to see him flapping his arms like some huge bird trying to break free from the snowdrift.

Once out on the road, Greg stopped and brushed snow off his jeans and the sheepskin jacket. Then he made his way in the direction of his wrecked car. After a few feet the falling snow closed around him. Finally, he disappeared.

Emily Rose took her thumb out of her mouth. "He gone, Mommy," she said dolefully.

"He can find his way back by the road," Julia said shortly. "Come now, girls. I need you to help me clean up the breakfast mess."

Neither child budged. "We're just going to wait here until he comes back," Deenie murmured, her nose to the window glass. "We have to wait to make sure nothing happens to him."

Julia counted to ten. She told herself it wasn't

smart to make an issue of it while he was still there. She hardly felt optimistic; she really didn't think he would hear any good news when he reached his car. There was too little time, the weather too bad, to hope that the bridge would be opened that day. From what she could see on their side, they wouldn't get out until the road scrapers came in.

I'll wait and see, Julia told herself, sighing.

She had cleared off the breakfast table and was cleaning out the bedroom fireplace when she realized the trip was taking longer than it should have. Emily Rose wandered away from the living-room windows to play with her toys. Julia cleaned out the ashes in the living-room fireplace and carried them out on the porch to dump them in the snow. Still no Greg Harding. Deenie stood steadfastly by the window, hugging the Christmas book to her chest.

Julia began to worry. If he was in trouble she really couldn't go after him; that would mean leaving Deenie and Emily Rose alone in the house. If he was hurt, trapped in the snow . . .

She'd only managed to get him to the house before because he was mostly conscious and could walk.

Deenie shouted, "Here he comes!" She dashed to the front door and flung it open.

Julia breathed a sigh of relief. Greg Harding came through the open door, accompanied by a blast of arctic wind, his hair covered with snow. He bent down and let Deenie help him carefully brush it away. Emily Rose threw herself around his knees.

"Damn, it's cold out there." He looked at Julia over Deenie's head. "Sitting in the Cutlass was like trying to stay alive in a freezer locker. And these local radio stations. I had to listen to what sounded like fifty years of Randy Travis and Porter Waggoner."

Julia helped him out of the sheepskin. The coat was so cold it was stiff as wood. "The blizzard covers pretty much of the southeast," he told her. "There have been a lot of accidents, people dying of exposure." He kept his voice down. "The interstate is closed, and most secondary roads are impassable. The state says it doesn't know when they'll be cleared. I suppose that dirt track out there doesn't even qualify as secondary."

"You're right about that." Julia hung the coat on the back of a chair to thaw out. "Then it doesn't look like there's a chance that the bridge will be open today?"

"What do you think?" He stood with his thumbs in the waistband of his jeans. "Well, Mrs. Stonecypher." He cocked a sardonic eyebrow at her. "What are our plans for Christmas?"

"The Christmas tree," Deenie cried. The girls were sitting at the pine table in the kitchen, helping the loan officer make a Christmas list. "Don't forget we still have to get our Christmas tree!"

"I really don't think," Julia said from the hearth, "we have to write all this down." The list was his idea; it even had priorities. As if there were time left for priorities. "We never do anything like that."

He was writing busily. "What about the Christmas tree?"

Julia took down the iron spoon to stir the soup she was making. "Yes, I was supposed to get the tree in town yesterday." He wasn't going to trap her on that one. "I planned on buying it before you came and ran your car into the ditch. That took care of that, I'm afraid."

He stopped writing and looked up at her. "With all the trees growing out here, you were going to *buy* one?"

Julia hung the ladle back up on its hook and wiped her hands on her apron. "Most of the trees that grow on the mountain are pine," she said evenly. "And some cedars, what people out here call 'cemetery trees.' Pines are lopsided and ugly, they don't make good Christmas trees, and I don't want anything that grows in a cemetary. I don't have the manpower to cut down a tree, anyway."

"You have now." He stood up, his eyes gleaming. "How about it, kids?" He started for the sheepskin coat on the back of the chair. "Shall we go out and get the Christmas tree now?"

Julia stepped in front of him. "Now just a minute," she said in a low, fierce tone, "don't tell my children what they're going to do! If you're going to do anything, you ask me first, do you understand?"

He stepped back a step. "Listen, Mrs. Stonecypher, I'd take what I could get, if I were you," he said, matching her tone. "Don't think I wouldn't rather be doing other things. Frankly, I'm due in Atlanta for a party in about four hours, then I'm scheduled to go on to a Christmas Eve gala at the Driving Club. Tomorrow I'm supposed to fly up to Charleston for Christmas with relatives. These affairs are something I look forward to all year."

"I'm not interested in your missed social engagements," Julia snapped. "I didn't invite you here!"

His eyes narrowed. "Let me put it to you this way, then. Since I'm here in the back end of nowhere, stuck in a blizzard, and all because you're a deadbeat, dear Mrs. Stonecypher, not to mention an airhead who spent her bank payments on trivia, I figure I can either sit in your living room with my feet to the fire and spend my time recovering from my concussion, or I can do my best to make myself useful for the sake of your kids. You're the one who's been making speeches about how much Christmas means to them, not me."

She drew herself up. "You didn't ask *me* about all this!"

"Why ask? I gathered, since you've been sulking around here all morning, that you weren't interested in speaking to me. Probably because we spent a couple of hours bundling before the fire last night."

"I'm *speaking* to you now," she hissed. "And I haven't 'bundled' with you—I don't know where you got that idea! It's too bad you're stuck here missing your social life in Atlanta, Mr. Harding, but I warn you—don't you dare say anything to my girls about what you're going to do to us when you leave!"

"What I'm going to do to you when I leave?" His eyes glittered. "Weren't you listening at all to anything I said last night?"

"Don't mention last night to me! I'll thank you to keep your voice down, do you hear?"

He glowered at her. "The kids and I are going out for the Christmas tree. Let me ask you politely: Are you going to join us?"

Enraged, Julia jerked the sheepskin coat out of his hands. "You're not going anywhere. You're not taking my children anywhere, and you're not going to wear my sheepskin jacket!" Her voice rose. "You ungrateful—*freeloader*, you can start wearing your own clothes!"

"That's fine with me." He was furious now; his lips barely moved when he spoke. "I'm going to cut down a tree."

"Here's your boots," Deenie said, inserting herself between them. She held up a boot in each hand. "Mamma, are we going outside to get our Christmas tree? Can Emily Rose come if Greg carries her?"

"I want my eyeglasses returned to me," he went on, "not to mention my wallet. I can't see anything without my glasses, and damned if I want to chop off my own leg doing this."

"Hah," Julia flung back, "don't tempt me!"

There was a pause. They were both breathing hard.

"Your mother is full of the Christmas spirit,

Deenie," he said, taking the boots. "Okay, what kind of tree do you want, pine or cemetary?"

Julia made a low, strangled noise.

They went down to the pasture in a small procession, Greg carrying Emily Rose with the understanding that once they chopped down the tree, Julia would carry her back. There had been a lot of wrangling about letting the children come at all, but selecting the various combinations of who would go with whom had finally come down to the fact that either everyone stayed, or everyone went. Deenie trudged along beside Julia, talking about Christmas Eve, how they were going to decorate the tree, and how they would all go to the barn at midnight to hear the animals talk.

"We're not going to," Julia told her. "We can't stay up that late. Now just stop talking about it."

"Why can't we?" her daughter persisted. "Lots of people stay up until midnight. People stay up to midnight on New Year's, don't they?"

"That's New Year's." She was watching Greg breaking a path through the snow with Emily Rose on his shoulders. "Not so far," Julia called out. "We don't want to get out of sight of the house."

She was somewhat sorry, now, that she'd been so unpleasant about his clothes. The tailored overcoat and wrinkled suit combined oddly with Grandpa Stonecypher's knee-high leather boots. Even from that distance the attempts she'd made the day before with cold water and laundry detergent on the blood spatters had left large, blurry, pink stains. In his splotched coat and business suit, he looked like an overdressed butcher. The cracked lens in his gold-rimmed eyeglasses made him definitely seedy. In spite of herself, Julia had to smile. Gregory Harding, bank officer, had been been transformed into the sort of person who, if he came into the Dalton bank for a loan, Bank Officer Gregory Harding would turn down in a flash.

"Please, Mommy," Deenie begged, hanging onto her hand. "It's there in the book about animals talking, and Greg said he'd come with us. *Please!*"

"Hush," Julia told her.

He had stopped ahead of them on a wind-scoured clearing where the snow was fairly thin. He bent and put Emily Rose on her feet. She was so bundled up, only her eyes and nose showing in a layer of wool scarves, that she could hardly keep her balance. Julia came up and quickly scooped her into her arms.

He turned to her. "Well, what do you think?" The carved planes of his face were red with cold. But dull light winked rakishly from the cracked eyeglass lens.

A few small pines marched down the slope. He indicated them with a swing of the ax. "Which one? Do we vote?"

Julia shook her head no. It was bitterly cold; her eyes oozed tears in the frigid air. Emily Rose had burrowed her face against Julia's shoulder.

He went down on his knees before a pine, lifted the ax, and swung experimentally at it. The sound of metal hitting half-frozen wood rang loud in the air.

Julia looked around. They were only a few hundred feet down the pasture. Behind them the house squatted in a grove of black-limbed oak trees, solid stone and enduring wood like the mountain itself. The chimneys gave out long trails of smoke, a cosy sign of life in the surrounding whiteness.

How silent it was! The snow blanketed everything. Under the moan of the wind, the mountain lay still.

"It's Christmas, Mommy." Emily Rose's muffled voice sounded against the sheepskin.

Greg had succeeded in hacking through the pine's trunk. When it started to fall, he wrenched it free. He rose with it in both hands, triumphantly, staggering a little. The tree was much larger than it had looked.

"You need me to help you!" Deenie plunged through the snow toward him. "It's our Christmas tree," she caroled, grabbing a handful of branches. "Isn't it beautiful!"

He held up a chilblained hand and examined it, frowning. "Blast it, do these pines have thorns on them? My injury rate is rising out of control."

Julia didn't answer. Hugging Emily Rose, she lifted her face to the snowflakes.

If I were floating in the sky above us right now like a helicopter, or an angel, she was thinking, *I would see us as a little group here in the midst of a snow-covered field. A man, a woman, and two little girls, like a calendar picture. Something*

called "Figures Cutting Down a Christmas Tree."
Or "Getting Ready for Christmas Eve."

It was the most curious thought, because, of
course, there were no helicopters or angels or anything else hovering over them, only leaden gray
clouds. But she could see it very clearly in her
mind's eye. The deep, glistening snow all around.
The old house on the side of the mountain with its
smoking chimneys. The snow-drifted fields. The
stands of green-black pines along the frozen
creek. And Deenie and Emily Rose and herself and
the bank officer, Greg, all bundled up in boots and
scarves and heavy clothes, their breath puffing
steam in the air. And the Christmas tree.

"Hurry up, Mommy," Deenie called.

Greg lifted the pine tree and maneuvered it under one arm. Behind him, almost hidden in the
branches, Deenie was struggling to hold up the
top. Like a lurching green beast, they started up
the snowy slope to the house.

Julia shifted Emily Rose to her hip and looked
up one last time. Somewhere above the storm
there were stars, and the sky. Tomorrow was
Christmas.

For the first time, deep down inside her in the
vicinity of her heart, Julia felt a faint surge of
hope.

Ten

AS JULIA HAD PREDICTED, THE PINE TREE was not only ugly, it was definitely lopsided and a far cry from the perfect pyramid shape of a greeting card tree. It was so off-kilter that the moment they put it in its red metal stand and stood it upright it fell over.

About the only thing one could say for it was that it was green, and fresh, and filled the house with a wonderful, resiny, Christmas scent.

Viewing the pine tree lying on its side, Emily Rose took her thumb out of her mouth long enough to say, "Christmas tree broke," in a sepulchral tone.

Greg got down on his knees to examine the stand again. "Not broke, just uncooperative," he muttered under his breath. "Like everything else around here."

"Pine trees always fall over," Deenie said soothingly. "They don't make good Christmas trees at all."

He lifted his blond head and looked at her for a few long minutes. Then he said, "Go get me a pencil and a piece of paper. We'll do this the right way."

Julia had watched the struggle for a while, then reminded herself she had Christmas Eve supper to fix. She left Greg and the children and went into the kitchen and brought out the mason jars of vegetables she'd canned in the summer, to make hearthside chicken stew.

It wasn't hard to see why the majority of main dishes of the last century were stews. It must have made for a rather monotonous menu, but the difficulties of cooking over an open fire in a limited number of heavy pots didn't make for many side dishes.

The old recipe, taken from Rachel Stonecypher's bride's cookbook, was similar to New Orleans creole chicken gumbo—which itself borrowed a lot from American Indian cooking. It called for cut white corn, the small green lima beans called butter beans in the South, tomatoes, okra, and onions.

All the ingredients were combined in a browned chicken broth. Then the chopped, cooked chicken and pieces of cornbread for thickening were added later. Julia always kept a few small packages of leftover cooked ham in the freezer. She threw in a handful of it while the vegetables were simmering.

The chicken and vegetable stew was hearty and flavorful, just right for their sub-freezing weather.

With baking-powder biscuits cooked on the hearth, and blueberry cobbler from the freezer, it was a good dinner. Not the one she would have cooked for Christmas Eve, when she usually tried something fancier, but good enough.

There was the problem of Christmas dinner. She had a turkey in the freezer, but roasting a turkey on a spit over the open fire would take hours, and she couldn't see herself sitting at the hearth in the morning, cranking away, while there were other things to be done.

Christmas morning, Julia thought with a slight shudder. Maybe by then the power would be back on; she crossed her fingers. The howl of the wind outside had been declining all afternoon; as darkness came on it was almost quiet. *I'll make up my mind about the turkey later,* she decided.

She busied herself with the stew, putting the big pot of ingredients on the crane, then swinging it over the flames. As she laid out the plates for the evening meal she caught snatches of conversation from the other room. Things there seemed to be having a hard time getting started. The hammering to get the tree into the stand a second time had stopped. So had the loan officer's terse orders to "Shift it" or "Hold it there." Her curiosity was piqued when she kept hearing words like "elevation" and "right angle."

Unable to resist, Julia went to the door.

For a moment she couldn't see anyone. The big pine tree lay lumpily on its side by the double windows. Then she looked down.

They were all on the floor. Greg Harding and

Deenie were on their stomachs in front of the hearth, Emily Rose tucked between them—her just-turned-three-year-old mind saw to it that she was literally always in the middle of everything.

The two little girls were dressed in the long-skirted wool and cotton plaid party dresses Julia had made them for the holidays, with frilly white collars and black velvet sashes. There hadn't been enough money for new shoes, as Julia had squandered her budget on the Royal Stuart tartan fabric on sale in the Walmart in Dalton, so both girls wore their imitation Reeboks. But they were angelically beautiful, as dressed-up as though they'd just stepped out of an old English painting.

Julia had found a black turtleneck for Greg Harding that she thought had belonged to one of Grandpa Stonecypher's Tennessee nephews. She supposed she'd made it plain that she didn't want to see him in Jim's clothes, so he wore the stained trousers to his suit.

He looked passable. Better than that, she allowed grudgingly. With his looks he could wear anything, including the ratty old turtleneck and the ruined pants to his suit, and make it look good.

"What you want to use is triangulation," he was saying. She saw the three heads, two fair, one golden brown, almost touching. He was drawing diagrams on sheets of paper. "You like numbers, Deenie, don't you? Right—what we have here is a kind of geometry."

Watching them, Julia felt a sudden, inexplicable pang. Her children seemed more than happy stretched out before the fire with this man who was explaining something—fairly advanced mathematics—they couldn't possibly understand. They seemed so comfortable. So satisfactorily *in tune*, the patient man and the two children snuggled up to him. It was baffling, when you considered they hadn't laid eyes on each other before a day ago.

Her emotions in turmoil, Julia turned and went back to the kitchen. There, getting ready for supper, she set the table in the kitchen with the Stonecypher English china and some pewterware: the Makim's Mountain branch of the Stonecyphers had never been affluent enough to afford a set of silver flatware. The big pewter candlesticks, with their many-times-used beeswax candles, went in the center, and she arranged red satin ribbon from the cake wrapping around them.

Not too many minutes later she heard Deenie and Emily Rose chanting, "The tree's up, the tree's up!"

She ran in to see. It was not only up but seemed solidly fixed. "Elevation" and "triangulation," whatever they were, had worked wonders. Julia admired it to everyone's satisfaction, then went to get the box of Stonecypher Christmas decorations from the hall closet.

Even with Deenie's paper chains and the cookies Julia had baked to decorate the tree, the number of Christmas ornaments was small. There had been years in the distant past when the Stonecyphers, like many in the southern Appalachians, hadn't bothered with Christmas trees, which were then still considered a "foreign" custom. Julia had bought a few glass ornaments, and there was a limited supply of handmade decorations from Jim's parents' day, when the house had been full with seven rowdy sons and three daughters. But the most interesting ornaments were the handmade ones whittled by Jim and his brothers when they were boys.

The oldest son, Roy, had been a talented carver, but Jim—considering that he was much younger —hadn't been bad at all, Julia thought, turning the little wooden figures over in her hands. There was real skill in Jim's carved figure of Santa holding a Christmas tree, made of white pine painted with water colors and a wire threaded through a hole bored in the top for a hanger. Reindeer and Santa's sleigh represented a slightly older Jim, in high school by then.

In the other room Deenie, who seemed to have taken charge of decorating the tree, was saying in an excited, bossy voice: "Too bad no electric lights. My teacher says in the old days they used to have little candles in little metal dishes that stuck on the tree branches. They lit them, and that was the only light they had. Only sometimes the trees burned down."

Julia went to the kitchen window to check the storm. Although it was dark, the snow no longer flew past like icy needles. She rubbed a spot on the steamy windowpane. The clouds seemed to be thinning. Now and then there was something like faint starshine that illuminated the white snowscape and the darker blot of the trees.

"This is my daddy's Santa sleigh," Deenie's

voice went on. "He made this when he was a little boy. And this is Santa Claus carrying a tree."

She heard the low rumble of Greg's voice responding.

"My daddy's in the hospital." This was Deenie again. "He's coming home someday soon."

Julia froze. Oh, lord, how she dreaded to hear those words! To know that closed look, believing its own unyielding dreams, on her little girl's face.

She started for the door. She had work to do for Deenie in the kitchen. She didn't need to make a big thing of it.

But in spite of herself Julia was hearing again all the helpful, friendly advice given in all those agonizing months after Jim had died. *Leave her alone, she'll grow out of it.* Or the more professional assessment, the counselor in Deenie's school: *Talk it over with her. The child needs to adjust to reality.* How often had she tried to do that? And how often had her child turned to her, locked away from her, believing what she wanted to believe?

"Your daddy's dead, Deenie."

It was Greg Harding's voice, matter-of-fact. The stranger in their midst.

Julia's shoulder hit the doorjamb hard. She looked around for them, frantically.

Deenie and Greg Harding stood in front of the finished Christmas tree. Deenie held his hand. Emily Rose rummaged in the ornament box at their feet.

The pine tree, Julia saw, somewhat dazed, did look spectacular. All Deenie's paper chains, Julia's cookies with the string baked in them so they could be attached to the limbs, the boxful of Stonecypher ornaments—the lumpy pine tree was cluttered, nothing on it was expensive or elegant, far from it, but it *was* beautiful.

"My daddy's not coming back?" Her daughter held Gregory Harding's hand and looked up at him with clear, hopeful eyes. Her Deenie look.

"No," he answered, "I'm afraid he's not. Hand me that paper chain, and I'll see if I can toss it up around the top."

Emily Rose held up a piece of paper chain from the floor. Pray, Julia told herself. She tried to take a step forward, but she was rooted to the spot.

"Do you believe in heaven?" her child asked.

"Do I believe in heaven?" He took the paper chain and threw it into the upper branches of the tree. It promptly slid down again. "Well, yes." He sounded careful, judicious. "I guess I believe in heaven."

Deenie picked up the paper chain and handed it back to him. "Is my daddy in heaven? Can he—can he love me like he used to from all the way up there?"

Julia saw him turn his head to look down at the little girl by his side. He looked somewhat bemused but perfectly serious. In her heart of hearts she thanked him for that.

"Yes. He loves you." He frowned, considering it. "Yes, I'm sure, from what little I know about it, that your daddy goes on loving you."

Julia put her knuckles to her mouth so as not to cry out.

"In heaven?" Deenie's expression was very earnest.

Greg took a fragment of paper chain Emily Rose was offering him. Julia saw now, through a veil of hot tears, that he was not all that casual.

"Yes, in heaven," he said. He paused, thinking it over. "I suppose if you believe in one thing, then the other follows logically."

"Oh." Deenie took the rest of the chain from her sister and handed it to him. "I'll have to tell Mommy," she said gravely. "I don't think she knows."

Julia turned and stumbled back into the kitchen.

When they were through with the tree, Deenie made Greg Harding stand in the kitchen doorway until she arranged an empty ladderback chair at his place at the table.

"That empty chair is for tomorrow." Julia kept her face slightly turned away, hoping her eyes wouldn't show she'd been crying. "It's Christmas *Day* dinner, honey, not Christmas Eve."

Deenie was too excited to listen. She took Greg by the hand and ceremoniously walked him the length of the big kitchen.

"Mother, Greg said Daddy's gone to heaven," she announced, "but he can still love everybody from up there." When Greg sat down, Deenie sat down beside him and patted his hand fondly. On his other side, Emily Rose quickly reached out to pat his hand, too. "Aren't you glad, now," Deenie said, beaming, "that we got him as our Christmas stranger?"

Julia looked at the man across from her. She didn't know yet whether she hated him for what he'd done.

He lifted his eyes to her. He said, his lips barely moving, "Let her go."

But that's what she was afraid of.

Eleven

AFTER SUPPER, WHILE JULIA CLEANED UP
the kitchen and heated water for the dishes, Greg
Harding went out to get more logs for the fire. He
seemed to enjoy the physical challenge of going
back and forth in the frigid weather until there
was a more-than-adequate stack of firewood for
the downstairs rooms.

"Well, what else?" He looked around the
kitchen. "How about my hauling some water
while I'm at it?"

Julia turned from the sink to stare at him. His
face was ruddy with cold, his blond hair disheveled. He was wearing his eyeglasses, but far from
giving him a businesslike look, the cracked lens
winked at her puckishly.

"What about your concussion?" Julia asked.

"It feels fine. Think of some more chores for me

147

to do," he said, picking up the empty bucket by the sink, "when I get back, will you?"

"There isn't anything more," she said shortly. "When I'm through here, the girls and I are going to go into the living room and sit in front of the fire for some Christmas music."

"Christmas music? Great idea!" He looked even more pleased. "Hold on until I get the water, and I'll be right with you."

"How do you know you're invited?" Some mean-spirited demon put the words in Julia's mouth; she was still thinking about his conversation with Deenie.

He turned to look at her. "You can't be evasive with kids," he said quietly, "they always know. I was only answering her questions."

Julia kept busy at the sink. "Tell me, are you married?" she said sweetly. "Do you have children? Is that what makes you such an expert with mine?"

He put down the water bucket and stuck his hands in the pockets of his once-elegant overcoat.

"No, to the first two questions. And I'm not an expert." He looked at her from under dark brows. "I remember what it was like to be a kid, so I speak from experience. I had more than my share of it."

Julia faced him, curious. "Of what?"

"When I was a child, my family hardly told me anything. 'Little pitchers have big ears.' If I heard that once I heard it a thousand times. Yet there was a lot going on that I found out about anyway —my uncle's first wife left him and ran away with a musician; my father's trusted comptroller embezzled a lot of money from the bank and things were desperate for all of us there for a while."

He gave her a wry smile. "I must have been a pathetic little brat, always trying to find out what everybody was so upset about. I think I promised myself then that when I was an adult I would always answer a kid's questions honestly."

Julia stood holding the dish towel, not knowing what to say. She'd thought of him as arrogant and unfeeling, but it seemed that wasn't so, at least not all the time. She almost wanted to say something to make him feel better. At least, she told herself, it explained the way he had acted with Deenie.

"I—I try to answer Deenie's questions," she said, trying not to sound defensive.

"I know you do." He looked down at her. "But sometimes a child just needs a different person to ask."

"A different person" to ask?

Julia stared at him, wondering if "a different person" meant that particular someone Emily Rose insisted on calling "Daddy" when she climbed into his lap. Or the total stranger that her daughter Deenie had claimed as a part of her Christmas, like Santa Claus or Good King Wenceslas.

Still, he *had* come as a stranger. He'd entered into their lives in the short time—a day and a night—that he'd been with them, and she supposed they all were changed by it.

Did she need a "different person," too? she wondered. Someone who would let her climb into his lap and rest her head on his shoulder? Someone who would give her honest, loving answers to all the things that she couldn't answer herself? It wasn't as silly as it sounded. Didn't she need to believe in someone, just like Deenie?

Julia was suddenly amazed at what she'd been thinking. *I'm going crazy,* she thought, looking away.

He'd been watching her. Now he said, "Julia," huskily. He stepped toward her.

She quickly turned back to the sink. Her hands were shaking; she almost dropped the dish she was drying. "If you want to join us, we'll be in the living room," she managed. "It's nothing much— since the power is out and we can't play Christmas carols on the tape player, I thought we'd sing a little. But it will take me a few minutes to get the Autoharp tuned up."

She knew he was standing behind her, not moving. A moment passed. Then she heard him pick up the bucket and go out.

He slammed the back door.

The Autoharp was in her bedroom upstairs, which meant Julia had to bring it down and warm it before the fire. That took a lot of retuning as the cold strings expanded and loosened. The girls seated themselves beside her on the sofa and waited, with only minor scuffling over who got the preferred seat on the end nearest the fire.

"This is better than television," Deenie told her, snuggling up. "It doesn't matter that we don't have TV tonight. I like it better when we do things like this."

"Well, this is more like the way people celebrated Christmas a long time ago here on the mountain," Julia assured her.

Some Christmas magic was finally making itself felt. The big living room was cosy. The kettle hummed and rattled with water boiling for tea. The bits of tinsel and glass on the big pine tree winked in the firelight. The girls in their long Christmas dresses were bathed in the golden-yellow light from the glass-globed kerosene lamps.

When Greg came in he took off his glasses, stuck them in his pants pocket, and took a seat in the rocker by the hearth.

"Is that the Autoharp?" he wanted to know. "I've never seen one."

Julia tuned the last row of strings. "They were very popular once up here. Like guitars were twenty years ago, when everybody wanted to be Elvis. Like those keyboard things are now." She strummed a few notes of the old German carol, *"Tannenbaum."* "An Autoharp is really a zither, with dampers that come down on the strings to make chords when you press these little buttons."

To demonstrate, Julia picked out the *"Tannenbaum"* melody and sang softly. The little girls joined her, singing, "O Christmas tree, O Christmas tree, How beautiful thy branches!"

Naturally, Deenie stopped singing to explain. "This is a Christmas carol my Great-grandaddy Makim used to sing," she informed Greg, "because his family came from Germany a long, long, *long* time ago. He spelled his name different."

Julia nodded. "Machem," she sandwiched in between the chorus. "Pronounced *Mock-em*. It turned into *Makim*, the way people talk here."

"Fa-la-la-la," Emily Rose demanded, sleepy-eyed. She tried to push the Autoharp away, leaning into Julia's lap.

Julia rescued it in time. "Yes, honey." She smoothed her youngest's curly fair hair with her hand. "We'll sing fa-la-la for the Welsh side of the family."

She strummed the first notes. Deenie began "Deck the Halls" in her clear, little girl's soprano, supported by Emily Rose's half-shouted obligato. Gradually they became aware of an uncertain baritone wobbling somewhere in the music, filling in forgotten words with an occasional "Hummm-um-humm."

She met Greg's eyes. The air had cleared a little. "I thought everyone knew the words to 'Deck the Halls,' " she reproved.

He grinned back at her. "Another one of those things my family kept from me. How about 'Jingle Bells'?"

They shouted—it was hardly singing—their way through the song. Sometime during the last chorus, Deenie slipped away and came back with her Christmas legends book. At about the same time Julia noticed that Greg had pulled out the yellow pad he'd used for the Christmas tree calculations.

She put down the Autoharp. "Are you making notes on this?"

He looked up, his hand partly covering the paper.

"I don't like you spying on us," Julia said. "I'll give you the words and music to the carols if you want them, I just don't want you using anything we do on Christmas Eve for your business purposes!"

"I'm not using you," he said.

Deenie had slid down to the end of the sofa to look at what he was doing. "He's drawing, Mamma," she cried. "That's you and me!"

Julia got up to see for herself. "Why, it is," she said, leaning over him.

The page was covered with small sketches of Julia playing the Autoharp, the girls beside her. Little pictures of her head in profile, her chin lifted, looking surprisingly beautiful. In one corner there was a portrait sketch of Deenie, wide-eyed, eternally inquiring, her lips slightly parted. Deenie to the life.

He shrugged. "I do a lot of sketching to pass the time. Always have, even in college."

"But it's so good!" Julia was amazed. Anyone who could catch a likeness with a pencil was a genius as far as she was concerned; it was a gift that baffled her as much as she admired it. "Did you ever think of making a living doing this?"

He gave her a crooked smile. "You mean, at county fairs, with an easel, doing pastel crayon portraits of people for fifteen dollars?"

That was exactly what she'd meant. But she

could see somehow that was stupid, and wrong. She felt hot color rise to her face.

"Wait," he said, reaching for her hand, "don't go. I'm sorry, I didn't mean to say that."

She shook him off. "I'm sorry, too," she said stiffly. "You can see I'm ignorant, and don't know about these things. I just thought with all your talent you could make more money than you could—well, more than you could giving out eviction notices."

He winced. "Touché."

She eyed him coldly. "I don't know what that means, either."

Julia went back and sat down on the couch. Emily Rose had dozed off in her corner of the sofa, the billows of her bright red plaid skirts making her look more than ever like a large, beautiful Christmas doll.

Deenie was at the other end, hollow-eyed with tiredness, holding her book to her chest. "Is it long, now, to midnight, Mommy?" she whispered.

"Oh, Deenie, stop!" Julia was still smarting over what she'd said about Greg Harding's sketches. She was still wondering where she'd been wrong. "We're not going to go through that silliness again, are we?"

Her child's face was adamant. "Please, Mommy, it's not silly, it's *real*! It's here in the book, all we have to do is go out to the barn. Greg said he'd go with us."

Julia didn't dare look at him. She sat down on the sofa again, pulled the Autoharp into her lap, and strummed a few bars of "Barbry Allen," humming to herself.

She was thinking that every time this man from the bank opened his mouth you could tell that he thought only of money and despised anyone who didn't; she'd been a fool to think anything else. He'd change their lives, all right! A few days with Mr. Gregory Harding and everything would have a price on it. He was probably wondering right now how much she was worth, playing the Autoharp and singing.

Across the room, he scribbled away, apparently working on more sketches.

Well, she needn't worry. Christmas Eve was almost over. None of them, she was positive, would be awake at midnight.

She was wrong.

At ten minutes to twelve, they left the house headed for the barn. Deenie had outlasted them all, sitting upright on the sofa before the fire, hugging her book of Christmas legends.

Even Julia had been dozing when the clock struck eleven-thirty. She dragged herself up in haste to help put on boots and coats and mittens and scarves. Emily Rose, roused out of sleep, was predictably cranky and uncooperative.

I wish we weren't doing this, she told herself. She didn't want to see Deenie disappointed, she knew her little girl's dreams would come crashing down around her when the animals didn't speak, and she dreaded the whole thing. But there didn't seem to be any way out. The argument, of course, was that their Christmas stranger, Greg Harding, had agreed to go.

It was so unfair. Eventually—tomorrow—he would leave and go back to his own world. It was all very well to make promises you didn't have to fulfill to a little girl. Like being there in the future to talk to, and comfort. No, you could walk off and leave her mother to do that.

But what happened to unlucky Deenie, of course, didn't involve anything *important*. Like money.

As they came out on the back porch they saw the wind had died completely. The night greeted them, still and silent and bone-chillingly cold.

As they started for the barn, Julia carrying a sleepy Emily Rose in her arms and Greg in front holding Deenie's hand, they could see the great storm had passed.

The black dome of the sky was faintly streaked with mare's tail clouds, pale as mist, as the blizzard blew itself away. In between, against patches of dark, the stars shone out—bright sparks of hope and light, distant and serene.

It felt like Christmas Eve, Julia thought reluctantly. It was so beautiful it tugged at your heart. The cold air caressed their faces; their breath billowed out like balloons of smoke. Julia carried an old kerosene lantern, Greg the flashlight. In the night, the solemn, majestic presence of the mountains and the beauty of the glistening snow was such that they gradually slowed to a stop, halfway to the barn, just to drink it in.

Lifting her head, Emily Rose murmured drowsily, " 's Christmas."

Yes, it was Christmas, as one always wanted to think of it. Vast, unearthly, and peaceful. The night dreamed on magically around them in snowy silence, promising the wonderful joy of Christmas morning.

At the thought, Julia's spirit shriveled.

Deenie turned to look back at her, hanging onto Greg's hand. "Oh, Mother," she cried, "it's a wonderful Christmas Eve. Can't you *feel* it out here?"

Julia stared at her daughter's eager little face, the faint star glimmer picking out the metal rims of her glasses. Her heart turned over again. It was Christmas, but there were no toys for Christmas morning. And, as Deenie was going to find out, no animals to speak, miraculously, in the barn.

It was time to turn around and go back to the house.

Just insist on it, Julia, she told herself. *Be nasty and mean! Everyone will hate you, but it's better than having your child hurt again.*

She saw Greg Harding turn to look back at her. She knew, with a sinking feeling, that he would go on to the barn, and that Deenie would follow him.

"Come on," Julia said unhappily. She shifted Emily Rose's weight from her aching arm to her hip. "Let's get this over with. I'm freezing."

They went on in silence.

The barn was even warmer now that the wind had stopped, but the smell of the animals was strong.

It was obvious they needed to be turned out in the pasture tomorrow, to let Julia put down new bedding.

It was dark and quiet. As they moved forward cautiously, no one spoke. General Lee, Daisy, and Miss Piggy were either asleep or huddled up in the warmest part of their stalls. Julia, balancing her sleepy child in one arm, put the old kerosene lantern on the ground, mindful of the piles of straw nearby.

"What time is it?" Deenie whispered.

Greg held the flashlight up to his wristwatch.

"One minute to twelve," he said in a fairly loud voice. "Actually, one half—"

At his words, a huge gray apparition, eyes rolling, lunged up out of the semidarkness. It banged, with a crash, against the stall railings like an enraged ghost—gigantic, formless, and filled with insane fury.

Julia jumped back, reaching for Deenie.

"Bwaaaaanh!" the monster bellowed, lifting its head and charging the rails again thunderously. *"Hawnk, hawwwnk! Byyaawwhn!"*

At the first roar, Greg had started violently, losing his balance. He fell against the boards of the General's stall, then slipped to his knees. The flashlight flew into the dark. That left the kerosene lamp as the only light. With great presence of mind, Julia dove for it.

"Screeeee!" The scream of a soul tortured beyond endurance ripped through the air. *"Reeee, reeee—RHEEEEHEEEE!"*

"Moooowunnnh!" Yet another ear-splitting re-

sponse blared through the barn. *"Ruuuuunh! Mwoooohuuunh! Moowhuuun!"*

The noise was deafening. Juggling both the kerosene lantern in her hand and Emily Rose on her hip, Julia tried to help Greg to his feet and out of harm's way.

"Don't get too close," she shouted. "The General hates strangers!"

He gave her an uncomprehending look. He got his legs under him and stood up, brushing fragrant debris from the knees of his pants. Julia grimaced. There was so much noise it was hard even to think.

Miss Piggy had jammed her snout against the rail of her pen so that the full volume of her squeals, aimed in their direction, could be appreciated. Daisy the cow merely lifted her head and trumpeted at the ceiling. General Lee's high-decibel brays were as ear-shattering as a freight train with its whistle tied down. In the midst of it all, a fully awake Emily Rose, who loved mayhem, was clapping her hands and laughing excitedly.

Deenie, Julia thought, shifting her youngest to her shoulder. Her heart was pounding.

Then she saw her daughter, muffled in coat, mittens, and scarves, standing directly in front of the maniacal old mule's stall. General Lee was throwing himself from wall to wall in a frenzy at the very sight of a hated male intruder. Who might or might not be the county agent. Or something worse.

Standing there, Deenie's hands were clasped under her chin in ecstasy, her face transported.

"Oh, listen, Mommy," she was saying almost prayerfully, "I told you the animals would talk on Christmas Eve! It all came true like I told you it would! I just wish we could understand their language!"

Twelve

GREG, ON THE SOFA BEFORE THE FIRE, slept fitfully.

He hadn't had that problem the first night; on the contrary, once he'd settled down, the combination of the bump on his head and sheer exhaustion had put him out like a light. With, he remembered with considerable pleasure, Julia Stonecypher in his arms.

But this night, Christmas Eve, sleep eluded him. After the episode in the barn his tired brain persisted in going over everything, trying to figure it out.

What a devil of a time to pick for insomnia. He was beat! He drew the quilt up over his head, stretched out his legs, and shut his eyes. After only a few minutes, he turned over, restless, lifted his wristwatch, and saw that it was already a little after one A.M.

Muttering under his breath, he gave up and lay with his hands behind his head, his feet propped on the sofa arm, studying the mountain pine he'd cut down for the Stonecyphers' Christmas tree.

The room was dark, lit only by the fire. From time to time some faint, hidden vibration of the old house, or an undetected draft of air, almost imperceptibly moved the glass ornaments, the carved wooden pieces, and quietly fluttered the handmade tinsel and gilt. The tree in its new beauty shimmered quietly, mysteriously, as it picked up errant sparks of light. Not the least of its charm was that it smelled like Christmas. Helped by the heat from the open fire, the air was gloriously pine-scented.

On a scale of one to ten, Greg mused, he'd rate this Christmas tree a nine. Make that nine and a half; all the homemade, homespun decorations were collectors' items, real Americana.

He was surprised at how much pleasure one could take in something simple like a pine tree. He'd always preferred his Christmases sophisticated and tasteful: elaborate dinners at the elegant homes of his friends, the theater, traditional parties in the company of beautiful women—no hard-drinking holiday bashes that laid you out with a hangover Christmas morning, no ostentatious open houses with wall-to-wall buffets and electrically lit reindeer on the lawn. In fact, at this hour, Greg remembered, he would have been at the Driving Club, celebrating the annual Bachelors' Christmas Even Dinner-Dance under the giant Norwegian spruce in the ballroom that the club had trucked in from Canada every year. The club's tree was guaranteed by its Toronto growers to be completely perfect. He happened to know because he'd been on the Driving Club's Christmas tree committee last year.

Yet here was a tree, he thought, eyeing it, that cost absolutely nothing except the effort to hack it down with an ax. As for perfect shape—it was more like an untrimmed hedge than any Christmas tree he'd ever seen. And the strange thing about it was that it still looked wonderful! In the firelight, it cast its own homely magic of what old-fashioned Christmases must have been like.

Magic.

He'd felt like he'd been under some sort of enchantment from the time he first set foot in this place, and magic was the only way to explain it. For the past day and a half what he'd been doing was so out of character that he knew he'd have a hard time convincing anyone that his actions reflected the man they all knew as Dalton Bank and Trust Company vice-president in charge of loans, Gregory Ailsworth Harding. Chopping down misshapen pine trees. Dandling little girls on his lap. Laying fires and hauling water. Not to mention making profound statements on life and death to a slightly mixed-up nine-year-old.

From the moment he'd opened his eyes and seen two little girls he'd thought were angels, Greg had to admit he'd been acting out a rather strange role. It was not like him at all. As for his going to heaven, he thought as he looked around the Stonecyphers' sparsely furnished front room, this was a far cry. Still, this place had come to look like something out of the last century.

Suddenly he had an untypically uneasy feeling. He'd seen an old movie on television, something with a dancer named Kelly—Gene Kelly. It was about a village that only came to life once every hundred years. He remembered the title now: *Brigadoon.*

For the past twenty-four hours he'd been living through something of the sort with Julia Stonecypher and her two little girls. They were four people trapped in an enchantment—if not in the Scottish highlands, at least its north Georgia counterpart.

Certainly the business about the animals was right out of a movie. They'd come back from the barn with a little girl who was convinced she'd witnessed a miracle. That on Christmas Eve the animals had actually talked.

Greg rubbed his face, tiredly. Thinking back on it, he didn't know why he'd interfered; Julia Stonecypher's kids were certainly her own problem. But he'd had the rather strange conviction that everyone should be entitled to their own delusions; it was a part of growing up. A part, unfortunately, his own parents had never paid much attention to. He remembered his own fervent desire to go to art school that had, very firmly, been deflected by his banking family and steered toward a BA in accounting and computer science, and, later, four years of law school.

Yet looking back on the whole episode, he'd had

no idea that a mule, a cow and a pig could generate so much overpowering noise.

It had been carefully explained to him that since all mules were sterile females the General was a *she,* not a he.

The bottom line seemed to be that the old mule hated strange human males. Had, in fact, tried to chew up the county agent at one time. Naturally, when one human male named Gregory A. Harding arrived on the scene, all hell had broken loose.

But this had been accepted as the real thing. The animals had spoken. The only trouble was, according to the oldest Stonecypher child, humans usually couldn't understand their language.

I'll put that scenario up against Brigadoon, anytime, Greg told himself.

He sat up and punched up the pillow before settling back with a muffled groan. So there they all were, shut up here in the house in the mountains together in a blizzard. The situation had its attractions and major inconveniences—both, in a word, Julia Stonecypher. Who was a remarkably good-looking woman; he had to admit she tempted him as no woman ever had. Not, Greg told himself quickly, that he was a compulsive woman chaser, far from it. But he had had his few serious relationships, mostly with gorgeous professional types in corporate law or in banking.

Julia was something entirely different, he thought, stretching out on the somewhat cramped couch and putting his hands behind his head. She was seductive. There was fire in her eyes and she could give as good as she got. He liked spirit in a woman. But in addition to all that, she had some fatal elusive something that—well, *got* to him.

He looked at his watch again. One-fifteen. He would never go to sleep at this rate. When he closed his eyes his mind raced with thoughts of everything—bank marketing schemes, the condo development, vacation fantasies to Europe or the Far East. Even about the mountains and hunting trips when he was a kid. He wondered if the old Stonecypher house had ever been under Indian attack. It was built like a fort, and there'd been some fierce fighting up in the mountains in the early days of the wars with the Creeks and the Cherokees.

He shut his eyes again. He wondered if he wouldn't rather live in a modern house in the mountains than in some very nice, golf-course-developed, security force–patrolled, exclusive high-income subdivision financed by, naturally, his own bank.

Disgusted, he turned over, yanking the blanket up under his chin. As he did so, his eye fell on the slightly trembling Christmas tree.

With a muffled curse, Greg threw back the covers and leaped to his feet. He groped for his jeans and stepped into them, then the too-tight bedroom slippers. He didn't know why he hadn't seen it before; he'd been lying there looking right at the confounded thing. The Christmas tree wasn't vibrating from drafts; someone was walking around overhead!

As best he could, considering the darkness, he found his way into the big kitchen and got the flashlight down from its nail. Then he went back through the main room and into the hall. He recognized one door as the bathroom, another, ajar, the bedroom. The third door led to an enclosed stair to the top floor.

The moment Greg climbed the stairs and came out into the frigid upper hallway, he regretted not taking his overcoat with him. It was bitterly cold here, shut off from the slight smoky smell of the downstairs rooms with their fireplaces.

He could hear a noise overhead that was definitely someone moving about. At the end of the hall there was a door. Beyond it, stairs climbed to the attic.

He wasn't expecting to find intruders. After all, who could get to them, snowbound, out here? He was cautious nevertheless as he ascended the attic's ladderlike treads.

His head came up into black, timbered spaces, and he immediately saw the light of the kerosene lantern. It sat on the wooden flooring, its crescent flame making tall, flickering shadows along the walls. Julia Stonecypher was sitting with her legs tucked under her, wearing the red robe, a blanket wrapped over that.

The attic was filled with the stuff one usually found in such places: old furniture, boxes, trunks, several beds and mattresses. She had drawn some of the old boxes and parcels around her.

He said, "What in the devil are you doing up here?"

He'd tried to pitch his voice low so as not to startle her, but she jumped anyway. He saw her cover what she had in her lap with her hand.

"I'm just coming down." Her hair was down, a dark, ringletted cloud around her pale face. In the light and shadows her eyes were enormous.

"Let me carry it for you," he said, reaching out.

She made no move to get up. She sat, her head bent, staring at the object in her lap. "It's a Noah's ark," he heard her murmur. "It's all I could find. That and Great-grandma Stonecypher's doll."

Greg knelt beside her on the attic floor. They couldn't stay up there in the unheated part of the house for long; it was freezing. But the tone of her voice disturbed him. Something was the matter with this woman who usually seemed equal to anything.

"Noah's ark?" he asked.

She held it up for him to see.

The toy showed the same type of skilled work as the hand-carved ornaments on the Christmas tree downstairs, but this had its own distinctive style. The ark's captain, Noah, a bearded figure in a Dutchman's breeches, his sons wearing old-fashioned broad-brimmed hats, stood on the deck with a plump figure in bonnet and shawl—Mrs. Noah.

With a quick movement of her hands, she opened up the hinged superstructure. Inside, fitted meticulously into each others' irregular shapes, was a veritable Rubik's cube of carved animals, all gaily painted.

"You have to learn to take them out right," she was saying, "as well as get them all back together. It's sort of fun. All the animals are actually a puzzle. They won't fit back into the ark unless you solve it."

He took the ark out of her hands and held it up to the light. The paint had lost some of its gloss along the sides, but it looked as though the generations of children who had played with it had done so with great care.

"It's a beauty," he said. "This thing must be more than a hundred and fifty years old."

"And the doll." She reached across him to the box on his far side. As she moved he caught the distracting scent of her hair and the tempting warmth of her body. Before he could do anything about it, she pulled back. "Emily Rose wanted a Barbie doll, but I never got into Raeburn Gap to get it the day you had your accident." She lifted the doll from its wrapping of yellowed tissue paper. "I don't know if this will do. Emily's just a baby, and she's rough with her playthings. The lace on the doll's dress is so old it won't take much handling. What do you think?"

She was actually asking him for his opinion.

Carefully, Greg put the ark down on the floor and took up the old doll. It had a painted bone china head, curled human hair, and kidskin body. It was elegantly dressed in clothing that must have been fashionable for little girls in the 1890s —a gray silk overblouse and gray silk knife-pleated skirt. The doll wore black kid button-up shoes that came to mid-calf and a floppy gray silk hat in the shape of a shallow bucket.

Another antique, Greg thought, examining it. It was worth several hundred dollars, if he was any judge. If the attic was full of things like these, Julia Stonecypher had possible assets worth a sum of money.

He started to mention the value of the toys, then remembered something else. "The Barbie doll? You didn't get into town for *what*?"

She drew the doll box to her and carefully replaced the tissue paper. "If you'll just hand me the ark," she said, not looking at him.

"What about your other little girl, Deenie?" The truth was beginning to dawn on him. "What was she supposed to get for Christmas?"

She reached for the doll. "Please don't raise your voice. I wish you hadn't come up here. These are just some things I'm going to put under the Christmas tree in the morning."

"Blast it." When she struggled to her feet, he got up with her, his hands full of the doll. "Julia—look at me. You mean you didn't have anything to give your kids for Christmas?"

She stooped to pick up the kerosene lamp. In the harsh eye of the light, her fine-boned face was even paler.

"I had presents for my girls, Mr. Harding. I meant it when I said Christmas means a lot to us up here." She turned to him, her mouth thinning. "Oh, I know, I'm an airhead and a deadbeat, just as you pointed out. But I had a used bicycle being repaired at Ace Hardware, and Emily Rose's Barbie doll at the Raeburn Gap Variety Store. I also had to get to town to deliver my pound cakes so that I could collect the money to get them. But when you wrecked your car," she said, "*you* fixed that."

She turned to go. Before she could reach the stairs he had her by the elbow. "Was that all you were going to get them?" he demanded. "A doll and a bicycle?"

She turned to look at him, her dark, beautiful eyes accusing. "How much money do you think I have? We're *poor* people, Mr. Harding, in case you haven't heard of the word!" She wrenched her arm away. "You've spent nearly two days with us, you see how we live. I don't know why you still don't understand!"

Greg stepped back. "Ye gods, no wonder you stole my wallet."

"I didn't steal your wallet! Besides, I gave it back to you, along with your glasses. You said you couldn't remember who you were, so I took it so you couldn't read your driver's license and find out and tell my girls you were coming to throw us out of our house!"

He looked at her in stunned disbelief. "Are you saying," he said hoarsely, "that when I landed on you here, when I wrecked my car, I kept you from going to town for your girls' Christmas toys?"

Julia shrugged. "Well, it can't *all* be blamed on you. It was snowing hard. I suppose they would have closed the bridge anyway."

"Great guns, don't be kind! After all, you've just told me I stole your kids' Christmas!"

Suddenly weary, Julia turned away. "What does it matter? I'm really worrying about Deenie. I'm going to have to tell her what I've been dreading—

that sometimes Santa Claus doesn't come. Or admit that Santa doesn't exist."

He stared at her. "She still believes in that?"

"Deenie hasn't wanted to know there's no Santa Claus, and a lot of other things, since her father died. The first time I've seen any change was today, when you got her to admit her father wasn't going to come back from the hospital." She stood, her shoulders drooping. "Maybe you're the one who ought to tell her about this."

He looked appalled. "Good grief, I wouldn't have had this happen for the world. Those poor kids." He was staring at her somewhat helplessly. "I've really come on like the stupid, inconsiderate ass I am, haven't I?"

She turned to look at him.

"Oh, you didn't have to put it in so many words," he said, bitterly. "But the message came through pretty clear."

"I told you, it really doesn't matter now."

"Oh, doesn't it?" He looked angry. "First I barge in here and notify you the bank is going to force you to move out of your home. Then I wreck my car and end up in your bedroom complaining about everything, effectively cancelling your family's Christmas. And as a result of all this, it's a matter of breaking it to at least one of your daughters that there isn't any Santa Claus, right?"

The way he talked, attacking every problem as though he could solve it . . . she almost smiled. Well, there was no solving this problem; he was seeing that now. She really didn't feel as badly about it; even if it was the magic of Christmas, he had made some things nicer just by being there.

She put her hand on his arm. "I have the old Stonecypher doll for Emily Rose. I don't think she'll notice the difference. As for Deenie—"

Unable to help herself, Julia leaned forward to look up into his face.

"What's the mat—" she started to say.

At that moment he reached out and, without any warning, pulled her to him.

"Julia, Julia, stop it," he said hoarsely. "You're trying to hold up the world all by yourself, and it tears me apart. I wish to hell I'd known—" His lips were muffled against her hair. "I know your husband didn't have any insurance on the motorcycle. And the police accident report showed he'd had a few beers—his blood alcohol content was over the legal limit. Did the other driver get a judgment against you?"

Julia had stiffened. Now she said between her teeth, "Please let me go."

He only tightened his arms around her. "Listen to me, will you? How much was it?"

She put her hands up between them and pushed. "This is none of your business! Are you going to let me go, or do I have to hit you?"

"How much?" he growled. "Are you still paying it off?"

She struggled only a few seconds more in his arms. It was futile, anyway. "Jim didn't drink," she said hopelessly. "At least he never drank around me or the children. He was depressed that we were going to lose Grandpa's house, and the welding shop wasn't making enough for us to live on. As for damages . . ." She looked away. "Mr. Whitfield settled for what was done to his Cadillac. Two thousand dollars."

Lines of anger showed around his mouth. "Why didn't you tell the bank that? All you had to do was sit down and write a letter, tell me what the situation was, that you needed an extension. You never even answered the notices we sent you!"

She pulled all the way back from him. "Would it have done any good? You've already told me you have a construction timetable to meet on those condominiums!"

Now that he had her in his arms, it was hard for Greg to think of anything else.

"Julia," he said desperately, "now that you know me—ah, what I do at the bank, I'm not going to let you struggle alone out here. I'm going to—" He was staring into her eyes, unable to come up with adequate words. "I'm going to—dammit, I'm going to kiss you."

To his surprise, she didn't pull away. But it was a kiss that neither one of them really expected. He wanted to go slow. At least in the beginning.

But what happened was entirely different. It was a kiss full of yearning and desire. And it went on for longer than he had planned, longer than was comfortable, or desirable. When it ended, they were afraid to look at each other.

"I don't think we should be doing this," Julia said abruptly. Her lips were damp and gleaming with his kiss. "I . . . didn't mean for this to happen."

"No," he said as if from a distance. "Nor did I."

Greg pulled away, trying to get a grasp with the logical part of his mind on what had happened. Kissing her, he was telling himself, was no big deal. In fact, it was innocent compared to some of his romantic liaisons in the past. He was suddenly glad that Trina, Marcia, and several others *were* in the past. The far distant past of several years ago. Because with that one simple, innocent kiss it was possible his whole life had changed.

An oversimplification, but true. You couldn't just blame it on Christmas enchantment; he wanted Julia Stonecypher. He wanted to be with her, he wanted to touch her, he wanted to make love to her.

He reached for her again. She gave a little gasp but moved willingly into his arms, her eyes wide.

This kiss was just as magical, he discovered. She opened her mouth to him and responded, first a little timidly, then with a surge of passion that turned to fire. When Greg finally tore himself away, he was vibrating with the power of it. He lowered his head to nuzzle the soft skin of her throat, breathing hard.

He ran his hand across her throat, her collarbone, into the soft curve of her breast below the opening of her robe and caressed the round, womanly warmth of her with trembling fingers.

Reluctantly, she drew back. "You shouldn't have done that." She put her hand to her mouth, her eyes dark, unreadable pools.

In answer, he reached out to pull her back up against him. "Something's happened, can't you feel it?" He pressed her against his shoulder and rested his chin on the top of her head. "Julia, I want to look after you," he said huskily. "Wait— don't tell me I'm crazy, I know how absurd this must sound. But I don't want you to have to fight and struggle any longer, trying to make ends meet up here all alone."

"Greg—" She tried to pull away.

He held her. "Just listen, will you?" he asked. "First, you've got to be provided with a house of your own. The Stonecypher house is going to be the inn, and I want you to be close by to be available for demonstrations of pioneer life in the mountains, the way you do so well. I haven't worked out a salary structure yet—"

She gently pulled his hands from her shoulders. "If you don't mind, I don't think this is a very good time to talk to me about your favorite subject, *money*. After all," she reminded him as she picked up the lantern, "it *is* Christmas Eve. And I have to go downstairs and do something about it for my children."

"That's what I'm talking about—a long-term basis." Greg felt like an idiot standing there talking when what he wanted to do was put his arms around her and kiss her again. "Aren't you listening? Julia, what happened here—" He followed her to the stairs. "That is, we can't ignore this. How do you think I feel? I'm just as surprised as you are. But I know what I want, and I think you feel the same way. The girls are part of it," he said, hastily. "I wouldn't want you to do anything without their consent, or participation. Or whatever it is you have to get children to do."

She held the door open at the bottom of the stairs. "It was only a kiss, Mr. Harding. It won't happen again."

"Don't say that." He tried to run his hand through his hair, again forgetting, and winced. "You don't think I go around doing these things casually, do you?" He caught himself. "Well, actually, there have been a few—uh, casual things," he said as she slammed the door to the attic stairwell behind him, "but nothing serious. Look, all that's minor, and hardly pertinent. I'm talking employment for a lot of people in Raeburn Gap. I'm talking putting you in charge of a cultural center to preserve the way of life still found here in the mountains."

Carrying the lantern, she led him down the frigid upper hallway. "Oh, you mean you want me to weave and sell artsy-craftsy shawls and tablecloths? And do genuine home cooking demonstrations, right here in the house I used to live in?"

He put his hand on the door and stopped her from opening it.

"Don't make fun of me, Julia," he said shortly. "You and I both know this way of life up here in the mountains is fading, and nothing is going to bring it back. I may be a money-grubbing opportunist to you, but I used to come up here when I was growing up. The mountains are part of my boyhood. I promise you I will try to save what I can. It's more than some others in my place would do."

"Why is it," she murmured, almost to herself, "that I always have the feeling you're going to sell me something? Or take something away?"

He scowled at her. "I don't think you understand what I've been trying to say. It's stupid to base anything on just one kiss, of course, and the spellbinding atmosphere of this place, but it's more than that. I've never felt like this about anyone in my life. And that includes the children, too. Although I freely admit they came as a total surprise."

They came out of the stairwell into the warmth of the downstairs living room. "Good heavens," Julia said, heading for the kitchen, "you're not going to offer Deenie and Emily Rose jobs, too, are you?"

He stopped by the sofa and stared after her. "All three of you," he said. "You haven't been listening. I'm in love with you, Julia. I want to marry you."

Thirteen

"IS THIS WHAT SANTA CLAUS BROUGHT me?" Deenie said.

Julia waved thick smoke away with her free hand as she bent over the skillet full of pancakes. One of the fireplace dampers wasn't working, and every once in a while a gust of wind from Makim's Mountain blew an acrid blast down through the kitchen and into her face.

"Because," her oldest child went on, "I remember I wrote Santa, Mommy, and asked him for a *bicycle.*"

Julia managed, in spite of her stinging eyes, to flip the pancakes out of the skillet and onto a heated platter. "Yes, you did," she agreed as she carried it to the table and sat down.

She'd been expecting Deenie's question ever since the girls had gotten up, at approximately five o'clock, to look under the Christmas tree for their gifts. But if Christmas Eve had been dream-like, even enchanted, Christmas morning was a cranky, demon-ridden letdown.

It was true the blizzard was over, and the sun had risen in a clear blaze of light. But instead of inspiring Christmas cheer for body and spirit, the glare seemed—to Julia, anyway—to make tired brains flinch.

She was filled with an almost irresistible urge to creep back into bed, pull the covers up, and stay there for the rest of the day.

No small part of her dismal feeling was due to the fact that, on top of everything else, she had to face Gregory Harding.

Deenie laid the ark down by her plate. Across from her, Greg was putting Emily Rose into her high chair.

"The ark is very pretty." Deenie's expression was carefully polite. "It looks like the Christmas ornaments Daddy made for our tree."

Julia met Greg's blue eyes across the table. In that moment she sent him the message that she was capable of handling this herself; in fact, she'd stayed awake most of the night thinking about what to say to Deenie about Santa Claus.

Before she'd crept into bed sometime before dawn, Julia had surveyed her handiwork under the Christmas tree and found that the wrapped gifts didn't look bad at all. Not lavish, but not skimpy, either. There were two white cotton blouses she'd made for Deenie for school, and a very nice ruffled pinafore for Emily Rose out of the same material. In addition Deenie got a set of ballpoint pens and drawing paper, her sister a new box of crayons. She'd also seen the gifts Deenie had made in school and put under the tree. One of them, she knew, was a pot holder for her, lovingly made out of knotted string. With the old toys nicely wrapped in Christmas paper, the pile made a good showing. A very respectable Christmas, after all.

Then, because she couldn't bring herself to leave Greg Harding out of Christmas entirely, Julia had taken two pecan pound cakes out of the freezer, wrapped them in bright paper, and put his name on them.

It seemed as though the girls tumbled out of bed only an hour later. Naturally, nearly everything was opened in five minutes.

Now Deenie sat staring down at her untouched breakfast. "I wonder if Santa Claus knew I wanted a bicycle," she said softly. "I wonder if he even got my letter."

Julia helped herself to a pancake and put a dab of butter on it. She wasn't hungry for even that much. Out of the corner of her eye she watched Greg cut another slice from one of his two Famous Stonecypher Family Recipe pound cakes, place it on his plate, then break off a piece with the side of his fork and stuff it in his mouth.

Julia was oddly embarrassed. The gift of two of the cakes from the freezer wasn't much, but he had raved about them. He was serious, apparently, when he said that he'd never eaten anything as good in his life. Now, she saw, more than half of the first pound cake was gone. The idea of that much cake for breakfast made her feel ill.

She turned back to her daughter. "The Noah's ark was made a long time ago, Deenie, by your father's family, whittled from wood the same way. That's why they do look a little like the tree ornaments." She saw she had her child's full attention; the solemn stare from behind those little gold-rimmed eyeglasses was unwavering.

Julia looked away. "Honey, do you remember the discussion with the children at school about Santa Claus, and what they said? That Santa is really the people who love you?"

Across the table Emily Rose lifted the china doll by its fragile silk skirt and shook it, shouting, "Barbie! Looka Mommy, Barbie!"

Deenie's eyes slid to one side. "It's not a Barbie, either, is it?" she said.

I'm not doing this right, Julia thought. She didn't want her child to feel betrayed, but Deenie's wounds ran deep; she never felt she got close enough to help with them.

"If my bicycle comes, then Santa didn't bring it." Deenie's expression was closed, unreadable. *"You* bought it."

"Yes, I bought it," Julia admitted. "I still have to pick up your bicycle at Ace Hardware. I would have done that two days ago, but Greg—your Christmas stranger—" She saw him look up at her tone. "—had his accident, and we couldn't get out before the bridge was closed."

Deenie turned to Greg with the same implacable look.

He returned it, coolly. "It was pretty hard for your mother to pay for the bicycle, Deenie. I understand she baked all those cakes to make enough money so you could have it."

Julia shoved the sorghum pitcher at him. "I don't need any help," she muttered.

He arched an eyebrow at her. "I don't need syrup for the pound cake, thanks," he said, handing the sorghum back to her. "It's delicious just as it is. What is this flavoring, anyway?"

"Flavoring?" Distracted for the moment, Julia couldn't think. "Oh—bourbon. The cake is flavored with nonalcoholic bourbon extract, because nearly everybody in Raeburn Gap is either teetotal Baptist or Methodist. But we do have some Episcopalians. I use the real thing for them."

"Fantastic." She couldn't tell whether or not he found that amusing. He turned to Deenie, who was struggling with the animals in the ark. "You can't get those animals back that way; it's supposed to be a puzzle," he told her. "Look, ask your mother if you can bring them over here, and we'll see if we can work it out together."

Julia put down her coffee cup, trying to squelch the curious uproar that was taking place within her and that increased every moment she spent with this man. She didn't know why she was upset; at least he was asking her permission. Why did it sound so much like a challenge?

I shouldn't have laughed at him last night, she thought miserably, *when he asked me to marry him.*

At the time the laughter had just come bursting

out because the idea was so preposterous—and, yes, because it had taken her by surprise. She supposed she could understand, now, how he had felt.

Deenie, the ark under her arm, had already slid in beside him at the table.

"Of course, go ahead with the puzzle." Julia got to her feet. Everything would be all right if she could look at him just once without remembering that devastating kiss in the attic. Part of last night had been spent thinking about *that.*

"I have to go to the barn to feed the animals, anyway," she told them. "Deenie, clear off the table before I get back, please."

Julia went to the sheepskin coat and pulled it off its nail. When she turned, she saw their heads together over the puzzle of placing all the animals inside the ark. Emily Rose leaned from her high chair, trying to get their attention as she waggled the Stonecypher doll by one arm.

They wouldn't miss her, Julia saw.

The sun on the snow was blinding. She stamped through the drifts thinking the world looked like a giant wedding cake, frozen and sparkling. A layer of white coated the windward side of tree trunks, piled up in the corners of fences, and decorated every branch, twig, and piece of barbed wire. She ran her hand along the clothesline and found it frozen stiff as a cable.

The first thing she did was let General Lee and Daisy out of the barn and into the side pasture. Daisy, big with her unborn calf, nevertheless took off down the slope, kicking her heels friskily. The General followed at a sedate trot.

"That leaves you, Miss Piggy," Julia said.

She left the barn door open to let in fresh air as she mixed Miss Piggy's mash. Then she raked out the damp bottom of the pig's stall and put down new straw. When she was through, Julia sat down and watched Miss Piggy dining elegantly with her front feet in her food.

She studied the pig thoughtfully, her chin on her hand. "I think he's out of his mind," she said to herself finally. "Either that, or he's playing some new game. I just can't feature any man proposing marriage after just a bare day and a half."

She sat thinking about it some more, not wanting to declare, even to Miss Piggy, what she felt when Greg Harding drew her into his arms.

It was too easy to think you could fall in love; goodness only knows she had been in love once, herself, for a long, long time. And when it ended she thought she'd never get over her pain.

"With people living with each other," Julia thought, "and doing everything and not even getting married these days, you can't tell me a man makes up his mind with just one kiss! I think he's just trifling with me."

She was trying to view it reasonably. But she knew in her heart she wanted to believe that Gregory Harding was serious—and yet everything argued against it. *Julia Stonecypher, the wife of a bank vice-president and well-known society tennis player?* Things just didn't happen that way.

Well, at least she didn't have to explain to her

children why she couldn't marry Gregory Ailsworth Harding. It was just too foolish to even
think about.

As she started across the yard she could hear
them coming; they were still a few miles away.

She stopped to listen, then began to run. Slowed
by the drifts in the backyard she had to half jog,
half slide down the last few feet to the driveway.

Her ears hadn't deceived her. Coming down the
road that led through the gap and over the frozen
mountains were three figures on horseback. No,
Julia told herself, holding her hand up over her
eyes to squint in the snow glare, not horseback.
They were mules.

She watched them. The three men were no
longer young but rather wizened, bundled up
against the cold. Their mounts approached slowly
but surefootedly, breaking a track through the
snowy road.

The old man leading had a scarlet scarf wound
around his chin and ears so that it covered most of
his face. Over it he wore the old-fashioned, floppy-
brimmed black wool hat of the mountains that
was seldom seen anymore. The man behind him
wore a knit cap so old its color had faded to gray.
The smallest man, bringing up the rear, wore a
yellow rain slicker cinched with a wide leather
belt and a baseball cap anchored to his head with
a knotted turkish towel.

Julia went out to the mailbox as the trio slowly
wound their way down the road toward her.

Mr. Mel Betsill, Julia knew, his brother Mr. Bert

Betsill, and the littlest man on the last mule was the remaining brother, Mr. O. T. Betsill.

She hadn't seen them in months. They were all three confirmed bachelors. Usually they came every Christmas to leave a gift of their best brand of white lightning elegantly packaged in a quart mayonnaise jar. Sometimes they left a piece of venison. Not even a blizzard could keep them away.

As she stepped into the road by the mailbox, Julia could see more clearly what the mules were carrying. "Oh, thank you," she murmured under her breath. She waved both hands at them.

"Merry Christmas, young lady," the man in the lead called to her. "You and the younguns all right?"

"Just fine! We lost the power and the telephone, that's all." He rode up, and she looked into his brown, wrinkled face. "My goodness," she marveled, "how did you get over the gap?"

It was quite a feat and he knew it.

He only laughed. "Used to do it in the old days, ain't no reason not to be able to do it nowadays. If'n you got good mules."

She could have kissed him—kissed all of them, for being so kind and wonderful. "Mr. Betsill, you know I can never repay you and your brothers for doing this," Julia began. "My little girls—"

"My pleasure, ma'am, a pleasure for my brothers, too." He dismissed thanks with a wave of his hand. "But if you're fixin' up a little something for Christmas, you can give us a mite of that fine Stonecypher cake you're so famous for."

Julia grinned. She had a freezer full, but she didn't tell him that. Just behind Mr. Mel's saddle the main part of Deenie's wonderful Christmas bicycle was tied on with rope. Mr. Bert carried one wheel with him, and Mr. O. T. the other.

Mr. Mel dismounted. "Yep," he was saying, "me'n Bert and O. T. was down to Raeburn Gap Christmas Eve, walkin' around and enjoying the sights, when here come George Quimby out of Ace Hardware, saying as how he had heard the bridge was closed up, and wasn't no way to get these Christmas presents out to your little girls. With you having such hard times these past two years, he didn't know but what you might need them pretty bad. So we loaded up Bert's pickup and took them up on the mountain. Then, first sign of clearing this morning, we saddled up the mules and put them at it. Took us the best part of four hours, didn't it, boys?"

The old men nodded.

"We see you and the children pretty nearly every Christmas, Miss Julia," Mr. Bert reminded her. "Wouldn't miss it for the world."

Julia couldn't thank them enough. When she tried to tell them how much she appreciated their action, the old moonshiners looked bashful. "You didn't forget Emily Rose's Barbie doll?" she asked.

"That dolly from the variety store?" Mr. Bert said.

"Sure didn't," Mr. O. T. put in.

"Got to have the baby's play pretty," Mr. Mel assured her.

The old men led their mules up the driveway

toward the barn. "You still got that old she-devil mule, the General?" Mr. O. T. wanted to know.

"Yes, the General's still here. But I don't think you'll have too much trouble if you'll just put your mules in the front stalls, away from her." As she spoke Julia could hear a commotion in the house; the Betsills had been seen from the kitchen windows. "Mr. Mel," she began, "I want to tell you about my oldest girl, Deenie. She still thinks Santa—"

It was too late. Her children burst out of the back door, followed by Gregory Harding in his turtleneck, stained trousers, and bedroom slippers.

The three old men viewed him with interest.

"I thought we might find you up here," Mr. O. T. called. "You the man from the Dalton bank, ain't you? Well, Dorothy Dixon's been telling half the state you was probably hurt and needed a doctor. Tried to talk the state police into flying a helicopter out here, but they been saying the weather was too bad for them to do that."

Mr. Bert Betsill was busy untying one of the wheels. "Little lady," he called to Deenie, "you know what I got here, don't you?"

Poised on the back porch step, Deenie froze, her eyes as wide and dark as Julia's. Then, with a cry, she launched herself at the three old men.

Mr. Bert laughed as Mr. Mel picked her up and swung her around. Mr. O. T. dashed a sentimental tear from his eye. "Makes it feel like Christmas, don't it," he said, nudging his brother with his elbow.

"It do now," Mr. Bert replied, huskily.

A few minutes later, Julia dragged the frozen carcass of the twenty-five-pound Christmas turkey out of the freezer. It wasn't too early to get started, especially since they were going to have *four* guests for dinner. The bird wasn't rock-hard; the freezer's temperature had risen somewhat, but it was still not thawed enough for immediate fireplace cooking. A bath of hot water first, she decided. And goodness only knows how frozen it would still be when she got it on the spit.

"You're going to have to help me with this," she told Deenie. "We're just like pioneers today, with a houseful of people to feed, cooking Christmas dinner in the fireplace. Since men don't usually do this, it's going to be just us."

"I'll help you, Mommy." She beamed, glad to be allowed to work at the hearth.

"Barbie," Emily Rose said from the high chair. "My Barbie doll!"

Julia had taken the Stonecypher doll away and given Emily Rose her Christmas present brought by the Betsill brothers. To her great relief, her youngest far preferred plastic-faced Barbie and her garish wardrobe.

Deenie was delirious with excitement as the Betsills and Greg Harding assembled her bicycle in the main room. Julia sat her down at once to learn how to turn the spit. Her child tried to pay attention, but the arrival of the old men with the gift that Santa Claus should have brought had set Deenie's mind working.

But she's happy, Julia thought, watching her. A

lot had happened in the last few days, but now her little dreamer seemed to be more satisfied. *I just hope it lasts,* she told herself.

She was working against time, shifting pots on their cranes, her face heat-flushed and her hair hanging in steamy wisps, when the bicycle assembly crew came into the kitchen.

Greg came to the hearth. When Julia turned to see what he wanted, he reached out to brush back a strand of hair from her face.

"We're going to take a break." He looked around. "I haven't been much help this morning, and I'm sorry. I need to talk to you, Julia, but I'm not getting much chance to do it."

Julia wondered if he knew what the Betsills were going to do outside. Mountain custom dictated no drinking in the house before the women and children. So the men "stepped outside" on the back porch for their little nip and an all-male chat.

"They're going to offer you moonshine." She saw his surprise. "You can do what you like about it, but I should warn you, the kind the Betsills make is a lot different from store-bought whiskey."

As she was speaking something obviously occurred to him. He stared at her. "I thought I'd seen those faces before! When I was in college they ran me off with shotguns because I was camping right on top of their still. I'd swear those old men are the same."

She had to smile. "If I were you, I wouldn't remind them of it." She asked Deenie, who was sitting at the hearth, turning the spit, "Are you getting tired yet?"

Her daughter shook her head. She'd been watching Greg and Julia intently. From her high chair, Emily Rose was trying to get Greg's attention by banging her Barbie doll on the tray.

Julia lifted a pot full of boiling potatoes from the crane. "Unless you have an iron head for drinking," she murmured, "I'd advise you to watch it. Moonshine is almost pure alcohol."

He grabbed a big pot holder and took the pot from her. "Would you care?" he said huskily.

Their eyes met. Julia's emotions had been simmering just below the surface all morning, and they suddenly erupted so that she couldn't breathe. She tried to take the pot back from him, and her hands were trembling so much that he saw it. He smiled.

She muttered, "Yes, I'd care." She was aware that Deenie, cranking away at the turkey spit, was hanging on every word.

"What?" He bent to her, pretending he couldn't hear.

His blond head was close enough for her to touch it with her fingers. The side of his face, his jaw, his handsome nose, were almost touching her own.

"Yes, I'd care," Julia breathed.

He turned his head, looking straight into her eyes.

"Why," he said softly, "when I long to take you in my arms and kiss you senseless, do we manage to have a big-eyed juvenile audience listening to every word, and a back porch full of overage moonshiners waiting for me to go out and get slightly bagged with them?"

"I don't know," she whispered.

"Neither do I." His hot blue gaze was on her lips, and she trembled with what he was thinking. "Maybe it's because we're living in a dream, a beautiful dream." At that moment the back door opened and a Betsill brother called out to ask if he was coming. "A dream where some damned thing," he growled, "keeps interrupting us."

He turned and walked away, leaving Julia standing at the hearth, her eyes half closed, her mouth uplifted, waiting to be kissed. After a few seconds she realized her children were staring at her. And the pot full of potatoes that should be slow-cooking in the embers was boiling away madly because he'd put it back on the crane.

Fifteen minutes later Julia had just started to fix the bread stuffing for the turkey when a terrible whirring noise assaulted the house.

"It's a helicopter!" Deenie screamed, bounding up from her stool.

Through the window over the sink Julia could see a black, roaring shadow pass over that side of the house and then turn to zoom across the side pasture. Every window in the house was shaking. So were the dishes in the sink she'd just rinsed.

She jumped when Greg stuck his head in the back door. His tawny hair was tousled, the tip of his nose red with cold, but he looked as though he was holding his own.

"It's a National Guard helicopter," he shouted

over the racket. "I think they're looking for me; they've probably seen the car in the ditch. I'll just go out and let them see I'm all right."

Emily Rose was screaming with excitement. Julia lifted her out of her chair. Deenie had already run outside without waiting for her coat or hat.

Julia tried to get Emily Rose hurriedly into her snow jacket so they could go outside, too, but the vibrations and mind-shattering roar of the helicopter hovering overhead and blowing snow in a thick fog was too much. Giving up, she threw her sheepskin jacket around both of them and carried Emily out onto the back porch.

"Just listen to that," Mr. O. T. shouted, his mouth next to Julia's ear. "They got a bullhorn up in that thing. What they're saying is the road grader's not far behind."

Julia couldn't hear a thing, only the *Rop! Rop! Rop!* of the hovering helicopter, and a blurry *rahrarharh, rahrarhharh* that she supposed was the pilot speaking over the PA system.

"Road grader's coming over the mountain that way," Mr. Bert Betsill bellowed in her other ear. "Can't open the bridge yet."

In seconds the helicopter circled the house, then flew off across the snow-filled mountain, taking its deafening racket with it. As it subsided, they could hear the faint, scratchy noise of the road grader making its way down the mountain road the same way the Betsill brothers and their mules had come.

They all peered at it; at that distance it looked

like a convoy. When the road grader topped the far rise, they could see two automobiles following behind it.

Greg had seen them, too. He turned and climbed the back porch steps with a suddenly somber expression, bringing Deenie with him.

"We've got company," he announced tersely. "I'm going to get my coat and boots. I won't be long." His blue eyes pinned her. "I'll be right back, Julia. Wait for me."

Julia supposed Greg would pick up his coat and boots and go through the house and out the front. The Betsill brothers had gone down to the driveway to watch the approaching road grader inching along, scraping powdery snow to one side of the road. The two black, shining Cadillacs followed close behind it.

Julia suddenly felt chilled, and it had nothing to do with the day's crisp, clear cold. She saw Greg come out onto the driveway at the front of the house and walk across the yard toward the mailbox. He had on his ruined cashmere overcoat and was wearing Grandpa Stonecypher's leather boots.

The road grader lifted its blade at the driveway so as not to throw up a wall of snow there, blocking it. Greg stepped carefully into the road. The first Cadillac slowed, then stopped.

Deenie came out of the back door and said, "I put on my coat, Mommy."

Julia was trying to catch what was being said. She strained to hear, but they were too far away.

"Looks like," Mr. O. T. Betsill observed, "them

people in the cars is somebody your young feller knows."

Julia saw Gregory Harding bend forward to speak to someone inside the first Cadillac. He gestured, saying something. Then the door opened and, abruptly, hands reached out and pulled at him. In the time it took to blink at what was happening, he disappeared inside the big black car.

The door slammed behind him. The Cadillac turned into the Stonecypher driveway, backed out, then started up the road across the mountain the way it had come. The second Cadillac did the same.

"Daddy," Emily Rose cried. She leaned out of Julia's grasp, her arms extended as if to snatch him back.

Deenie had watched, astonished. "Mother?" she cried, looking up at her.

Julia had been staring open-mouthed, too. Greg Harding was going back to the world she knew so little of—the moneyed world of country club parties, holiday trips, and beautiful, well-dressed women—without even a backward look. For a moment, she felt strangely frightened; then something shriveled up inside her and died.

Just wishing for something doesn't make it come true. The very thing she'd tried to tell Deenie. Perhaps it applied to Gregory Harding.

A wisp of smoke, breaking into her shock, drifted past Julia's nose. She smelled something nasty and burning.

"The turkey!" she cried.

* * *

The kitchen was filled with dense, greasy smoke. Julia, coughing, holding Emily Rose on one hip, managed to get to the fireplace and pull the spit out of the fat-blazing fire.

The Betsills crowded in the back door after her.

"Don't fret, little lady," Mr. Bert consoled her as he followed her to the sink and watched her deposit the charred, half-frozen turkey in it, "we've brought some venison." A fragrant cloud of mountain redeye wafted around him as he breathed. "We can cook that up for you in no time."

Suddenly, there was a faint *rrrrrrrrr* from the refrigerator in the utility room. Then a *CLUNK!* from some unseen electric motor.

"Mamma!" Deenie cried, excited. Not knowing what it was all about, Emily Rose screamed, too.

The kitchen lights came on. The microwave, which Julia discovered she'd left turned on, promptly began its empty, businesslike whirring.

In the living room, where little hands had worked at its knobs during the power outage, the television set suddenly blasted with a larger-than-life Christmas Day football game from Miami, Florida.

"It's all right, Mr. Bert." Julia sank into a chair at the table and put a still-shrieking Emily Rose on her feet. "Now that the microwave's working," she said over the noise, "I think we'll just have some pizza from the freezer for Christmas dinner."

Her oldest daughter threw herself into Julia's lap. "Mommy, my bicycle that Mr. O. T. and Mr. Bert and Mr. Mel brought me is all fixed. Can I take it outside?" She saw Julia's abstracted look and tugged at her sleeve. "It makes people nicer to each other, doesn't it, being Santa Claus for little kids? Especially"—she gave her howling sister a sidewise glance—"when you can't let *little* kids know what you're doing?"

"Yes," Julia said.

Wait for me, he'd told her. *I'll be back.*

Somehow—and she didn't know the reason why —she feared that wasn't going to happen.

Fourteen

TWO DAYS AFTER CHRISTMAS THE MAKIM'S Mountain bridge was still closed, so Julia made the trip over the gap with Deenie and Emily Rose to the hamlet of Nancyville and the 7-Eleven to get a gallon of fresh milk and hear stories of the blizzard.

It was still very cold, and the sun on the gleaming snowfall was so bright that Julia had to search out her summer sunglasses and wear them to drive the car. She found a number of mountain people had gathered in the 7-Eleven, which Julia remembered as the old Nancyville General Store, to exchange their news of the storm.

It was the worst in twenty-five years, everyone agreed, and there'd been some near tragedies: a young couple coming across the foothills in their automobile from Ellijay on Christmas Eve got caught in snowdrifts and nearly froze to death before they were rescued early Christmas Day. Farmers lost livestock that they hadn't been able to get under shelter before the big storm hit. Many wells were out; the pumps had burst with the cold. Telephones still were out of order on the Nancyville side of the mountain, although most of the electric power had been restored.

It didn't really come as a surprise to Julia that people in Nancyville had heard of her visitor, the man from the bank who'd wrecked his car right in front of her house and then had to spend all of Christmas with her and her little girls.

"Greg was very nice," Deenie piped to the interested 7-Eleven listeners, "he was our Christmas visitor. We had a chair waiting for him at the table, and he slept in—"

"Daddy," Emily Rose took her thumb out of her mouth long enough to say. "My Greg daddy!"

"It's time to go, girls," Julia said. She didn't dare look at the faces as she herded the girls to the door.

She knew what the Nancyville people were thinking, and it was all true, according to the way they saw it. Yes, she'd had a very good-looking man stay in her house during the blizzard, and she supposed she'd even had what people thereabouts called a "little fling." Gregory Harding had been attentive in his own way, said nice things to her, and he'd even kissed her.

Let them make of that what they would, Julia thought, her cheeks burning.

"And he's coming back," Deenie said loudly as

they went out. "He said he would, didn't he, Mommy? Didn't you hear him say that?"

Julia pushed her ahead. "Yes, Deenie, we all heard him say that."

But would Gregory Harding really come back, as he'd said?

Julia had wondered about it ever since she'd seen him disappear in the black Cadillac without even looking back. Now she didn't know what she believed. She'd told herself a hundred times the telephones were still out and he couldn't call; the only way onto the mountain, if someone wanted to visit, was the roundabout fifty-mile detour through Nancyville and then over the gap. The dirt roads were still slick and frozen. And it was almost impossible to get to her house from the bank in Dalton, using that way.

None of that made her feel any better.

She wished she could stop thinking about it, yet the very way he'd left Christmas Day left so much hanging. In a frenzy of wanting to forget, she threw herself into her housekeeping, airing out the downstairs rooms, cleaning out the fireplaces, carrying the ashes to put in the driveway. Gradually, she put away the things that reminded her of their strange and wonderful Christmas. Because there was no reason, really, to expect Gregory Harding to come back.

Still, it didn't help when she collected the things he'd left behind: one partly eaten, gift-wrapped, Famous Stonecypher Family Recipe pound cake, his nicely dried-out, Italian-made leather oxfords, his black silk socks, the bloodstained shirt and expensive suit jacket. Looking at them, she remembered his touch, his kiss, the look in his eyes. What he'd said to her. That he wanted to marry her.

Holding his black socks in her hand, Julia shed a few bitter tears. It was the worst sort of daydream, to think that she could be smitten with someone like Greg. But that didn't keep her heart from aching over it.

Quickly, she dumped his things in a box and told herself to be practical. Gregory Harding, bank officer, country club tennis player, had no place in her life. He was a man accustomed to wealth and fine homes, handsome, educated, cultivated, talented—all those things she, Julia Stonecypher, *wasn't*. As far as the way he'd acted during Christmas, he was just making the best of a bad situation. He'd been shut up for nearly two whole days in a snowstorm with a widow and her little girls— a little flirting was certainly harmless enough. How else did you expect somebody like that to pass the time?

In the end, Julia was thoroughly miserable. The truth was, she'd fallen in love. Talk about humiliation! She'd never thought she could make such a fool of herself. When the telephone came back on, she intended to call the bank and tell them she was sending all his belongings on to them in a package.

The next day the county road crew opened Makim's Mountain bridge and the mailman came through from Raeburn Gap for the first time since the day before Christmas Eve.

There was such a pile of mail that Julia sat down on the front steps with Emily Rose to sort through it, while Deenie, still on her Christmas holidays from school, rode her bicycle up and down the driveway.

"Mommy, watch me!" she called.

Julia looked up and smiled. Inside, her heart was sinking. Among the bills was a letter she recognized at once from the Dalton bank stationery. She ripped it open.

It read: *"Due to the special circumstances of your rental and your failure to—"*

It was not anything to get upset about; the letter only told her again what she already knew. That the bank wanted her to vacate the Stonecypher farm, house and premises, by the first week of January.

But it was signed *Gregory A. Harding.*

Emily Rose had pulled off her mitten to rummage in Julia's lap among the bills. "Mommy give me letter," she demanded.

You see, Julia told herself, *it was all a magical dream. And now it is gone.*

It helped her state of mind that she'd already made arrangements with the Betsill brothers before they left to take General Lee. The mule would have a good home with them. Mr. Bert Betsill solved her other problem by promising that the next time he went to the livestock auction he would come by and pick up Daisy and take her there to sell her. That left only Miss Piggy.

Suddenly she felt like she wanted to cry.

Don't be an idiot, she scolded herself. She

hadn't expected a thing from Mr. Gregory A. Harding, so nothing was lost. And his cold, impersonal letter, written as though he'd never even set eyes on her, or Deenie or Emily Rose, was no surprise. He was past history, a part of the Christmas enchantment that had held them all during the blizzard. Hadn't he even said as much? "A dream, a beautiful dream," he'd called it Christmas morning in the kitchen.

"Mother, look at me," Deenie shouted again as she tore down the driveway on her bicycle.

Julia dutifully lifted her head to watch. Since Christmas—and the bicycle—her dreamy little girl had become an energetic whirlwind, boisterous around the house, even more patronizing if possible toward her younger sister, especially about Santa Claus and other similar subjects. It was a little unbelievable, but she had watched it happen.

"Very good," Julia called as Deenie made a wobbly turn by the mailbox.

Well, Julia thought, at least the letter showed where Greg Harding stood. Now she could put all this behind her.

The telephone was ringing inside the house. It had been out so long it took Julia a moment to realize what it was. Then, telling Emily Rose to stay on the top step and put her mittens back on, she gathered the mail and went in.

It was Dorothy Dixon.

"I just wanted to be the one to call you now that the phone is working," her neighbor said.

Julia told Dorothy a little of what had happened during the storm, while she tried to keep an eye on Deenie and Emily Rose through the living-room window.

"The bridge is opened up so the mailman can come through," the other woman said. "I hope they keep it open for the school bus next week. Things are getting back to normal, fast."

Yes, things were getting back to normal. From where she stood Julia could see the snow melting under the eaves, forming a long, dripping icicle. A crystal drop fell from its narrow tip even as she watched. A freeze never lasted long in the southern mountains; in a day or two the snow would melt away. Except for a lot of mud, you wouldn't be able to tell there had ever been a blizzard.

Just as dreams melt. Suddenly Julia wanted to confide in Dorothy, ask her what you did to forget someone like Greg Harding, a man you could never have. In all the years she'd known her, she really couldn't imagine what her friend would say to *that*.

More traffic was coming over the bridge and up the road; Julia could hear it. Leaning to look through the glass, she saw a pickup truck.

Mr. Bert Betsill, she was sure. Of course he hadn't been able to get in touch with her while the telephone lines were still down, but she hadn't expected him to come for Daisy so soon. Her second thought was that she'd better get the girls out of the way, or a flood of tears over old Daisy would drown out the rest of the morning.

"I've got to go, Dorothy," Julia said quickly.

But by the time she got to the front porch steps she could see it was not Mr. Bert Betsill. The Ford pickup was much too new and its paint too shiny. Deenie's bicycle was lying on its side and Deenie was nowhere in sight. Emily Rose was still sitting on the top step where she'd been told to stay, but she was wailing unhappily.

Julia watched a tall, tawny-haired man in a finely tailored gray pinstripe suit come around the truck from the driver's side. Her heart leaped. She stood rock still as he went to the rear of the truck, trailed by her adoring oldest child, and let down the tailgate.

Julia wanted to run away. Instead, she snatched up Emily Rose like someone grabbing for a life jacket in a stormy sea, and held onto her.

Why did he always have to be so elegantly dressed? She was wearing the old sheepskin jacket and jeans, her flyaway hair blowing around her face so that she could hardly see. Then he looked up and found her standing there at the top of the steps. His gaze raked her like blue flame.

"I like your new eyeglasses," Deenie was saying as she pulled on his hand. "They're just like mine."

Yes, he had new eyeglasses, Julia thought, a little crazily. But those familiar features, that wide, tender mouth that had kissed her, were still the same. Her heart was racing so fast she had to remind herself how much she hated him. She'd stuffed his latest letter about vacating the premises in her pocket; she still had it with her.

He started toward her. "I'm sorry I took so much time. Several things delayed me, and I couldn't call you because your phone was still out. It's almost impossible to special order the World Book encyclopedia on a rush basis. But I thought Deenie could start on it now, during Christmas break while school is out."

"Good morning, Mr. Harding," she said flatly.

Emily Rose tried to lurch from her arms, her mittened hands held out mutely to Greg. Julia hauled her back.

He stopped. "Yes, good morning. Julia," he said in a different voice, "let me explain about the other day."

"You don't have to explain anything," she said. "It's not important."

"Not important?" He looked genuinely confused. "But it is. My father and brother were . . . very concerned about where I'd been in the blizzard, not having heard from me. My father got a little carried away, dragging me into his car like that. He's a difficult man to deal with. We had a fight about it, but it's all straightened out."

Deenie had climbed into the back of the pickup. "Mother," she called, "you should see what Greg brought. There's *boxes* and *boxes* back here!"

"Since I wasn't able," he went on, "to give anybody anything for Christmas for obvious reasons, I thought I'd take care of that now."

Julia's face froze. He was so money-minded—did he really think he could pay her back? He must have a guilty conscience about leading her on!

"You don't have to bring us anything." She had to shift Emily Rose, who was still holding out pleading arms to him, to her hip. "We were glad to put you up during the storm. You don't have to pay us."

"Books and books!" Deenie yelled from the truck bed. She was going from box to box. "I *love* books. And this box has a whole bunch of dolls in it!"

"Actually, they're marionettes." He stared at Julia, frowning. "I liked marionettes when I was a kid. I thought if Emily Rose likes dolls, probably she has some talent that way."

His voice faded away as he saw Julia take the crumpled letter from the bank out of her pocket. She held it out to him. He took the letter and opened it.

He groaned.

"Lord, this was mailed a week ago. The blizzard delayed it. You can't blame me for this now." He took another step toward her. "You don't really think this still applies, do you?"

"I don't know what I think. You say one thing and do another. After all you said to me during Christmas, now you write me this letter and tell me to leave!" As he started toward her again she cried, "No, stop right there! I don't know what you want from us, but we don't need your presents. You can take them and whatever else you've got in your truck and leave us alone!"

She would have turned away, but he reached out and caught her by the arm. As he did so, Emily Rose clamped her mittened hands around his neck. "Daaaady," she breathed.

Julia pulled at her. "Emily Rose, let go."

Her daughter's clutch on him locked them together. His blue eyes, so close now, were devouring her.

She tugged at Emily again. "I'm not going to stand here like this. Please let go of her."

"I'm not holding her, she's holding me. They're not just Christmas presents," he said huskily, "they're everything I want to give you, and yet they're not enough, Julia."

"Emily Rose, let go of him," Julia said through clenched teeth.

With some difficulty, since Emily Rose had her arms around his neck, he reached into his suit jacket and pulled out a folded piece of paper. He shook it open.

"I made some notes while I was here, based on what I saw you could use. For instance, I chose the World Book encyclopedia for Deenie because I had a set when I was a kid, and it has enough information, I think, to keep her busy this year." Emily Rose's squirming shoved his glasses to one side; he pushed them back up on his nose. "I've been swamped at the bank the last couple of days, but I did have a chance to look up my Hammacher Schlemmer catalogue, and there's an electric spit available. It's expensive but it seems there are actually a number of people cooking in fireplaces these days."

"Daaady," Emily Rose crooned. She patted his cheek. "My Daddy Greg."

He grabbed her hand quickly and held it. "Hammacher Schlemmer sent it air express; it's in one of the boxes labelled—" He looked at the note on his list. "Hammacher Schlemmer, naturally enough. And there are, um, some other items for you." He couldn't meet Julia's eyes. "Red nightwear in lace and, ah, different trimmings."

Julia stared at him. "Red nightwear in lace and different trimmings? You put *that* on your list?"

Now his eyes narrowed, determined. "Julia, I've worked on this for two days since I got back. What's in the truck is just not a random selection that anyone could have picked out, it's been carefully thought out in spite of the fact that the bank's been a madhouse and I haven't had much time. But you must know by now what you and the girls mean to me, what plans I hope to have for us. My whole life changed during the days I spent here. Are you going to marry me?"

Julia sucked in her breath. *"What?"*

Deenie danced around them. "Are you going to marry him, Mother, are you? Are you going to marry Greg? Please say yes!"

He spared a moment to look down at her. "What's happened to her?"

Julia shook her head. "I don't know, you tell me." She tried to hold onto Emily Rose, who was clinging to him like a limpet. "Since Christmas she seems to be a different child."

"Ah, Julia," he murmured. His arms were around both of them now. "I love you. I'm not asking you to do anything you don't want to do, am I?"

Julia's resistance was draining away. "It wouldn't work, I don't know why you think it would," she protested feebly. "I'm a Makim's Mountain widow with two children. You know what people would say. We're not the same sort at all!"

Even as she said it she had a sudden, vivid memory of Christmas Eve when they went to cut down the pine tree in the storm. And how they looked, the four of them, a woman and a man and two little girls, standing in the snowy field. In that time and place Julia remembered thinking that angels, or someone in a helicopter, could look down and see them, this happy family, cutting down their tree for Christmas. She remembered, too, that feeling of joy, and hope.

Because they had been a family, Julia realized. And happy, in spite of the differences, in spite of the past.

She tried to pull away. "Wait, I think we ought to go slow, at least until—"

"No," Deenie shouted, circling them, "let's get married now!"

He pulled her to him.

"Julia, don't fall back on your confounded mountain pride. I have something to tell you. I took part of that cake you sell away with me to see if I could get some sort of marketing survey done on it. The upshot is that the bank is impressed and will finance you in your own baking company, but of course it's too soon to come up with concrete numbers until we see where we're going. Or you're going. However, some friends of mine think that a line of Stonecypher pecan pound cakes, in conjunction with what we're going to do at the Appalachian Lodge, has great promise. Look, don't forget Claxton fruitcakes," he told her quickly, "and what a success that company has been right here in the state. Are you listening?"

Julia was listening. She pulled back to look up at his handsome, intent face, the strands of fair hair that fell over his forehead. She wondered if it was because he stayed so busy that he kept forgetting to get a haircut.

And there was the list in his free hand. Another list. She had a feeling there would always be one. She knew that was what made him so dear to her.

"If everything works out right," he was saying, "you'll be independently wealthy. Give or take a few start-up hiccoughs." He cocked one eyebrow, waiting for approval.

She smiled at him tentatively. "Don't forget I'm an airhead and a deadbeat."

He winced. "Don't throw my words back at me, please. Look, I don't want you to worry unnecessarily. I'll get you specialty baking consultants to steer you through the first few months." He peered at her. "Julia? What's the matter?"

She was only smiling at him through a happy haze of tears. He had his own way of showing it, but she knew he did love her. "I love you, too," she murmured. "I just don't think you'll ever know all the reasons why."

"Yay," Deenie whooped. She threw her arms around both of them. "This was the best Christmas! Oh, it was, it made everybody so happy." She lowered her voice, nodding at Emily Rose. "Even though now, of course," she confided in a whisper, "I'm really too *old* to believe in Santa Claus."

Julia turned her face into Greg's shoulder and felt his arm tighten around her.

"I'm glad I'm not." Deenie was right about this Christmas; there would never be another one like it. "Oh, yes," Julia whispered fervently, "I'm so glad *I'm* not too old to believe in him."

When the young woman awakens in the hospital,
everyone recognizes her as Amanda Farraday, the
selfish socialite wife of Dr. Brent Farraday—yet her
clouded memory cannot recall her glamorous
lifestyle, nor can she understand why her
handsome, desirable husband detests her. The
secret lies buried in her true past—a past she must
now uncover, or lose her heart's deepest desire...

SHATTERED ILLUSIONS

A NOVEL IN THE BESTSELLING TRADITION OF SANDRA BROWN BY

LINDA RENEE DeJONG

Heading for a new life in California across the untracked mountains of the West, beautiful Anna Jensen is kidnapped by a brazen and savagely handsome Indian who calls himself "Bear." The half-breed son of a wealthy rancher, he is a dangerous man with a dangerous mission. Though he and Anna are born enemies, they find that together they will awaken a reckless desire that can never be denied...

SECRETS OF A MIDNIGHT MOON

Jane Bonander

IN THE BESTSELLING TRADITION OF BRENDA JOYCE

ROSAMUNDE PILCHER

the acclaimed author of the landmark bestseller,
THE SHELL SEEKERS,
now takes you on a new and unforgettable journey
of homecomings and heartbreaks, friendships,
forgiveness and love.

SEPTEMBER

the #1 national bestseller, is a book to
cherish—a novel you will never forget.